TRIAL

Narative Philosophy

D.C. Reed

D.C. Reed Publishing LLC

ISBN:
Digital: 978-1-7372419-0-4

Physical: 978-1-7372419-1-1

Cover design by: DC REED
Library of Registration Number: TXu002214504
Printed in the United States of America

*To all of those who push for the truth and
don't let the easy stop them.*

"Learn as if you were to live forever...."

GANDHI

CONTENTS

TRIAL

A Philosophical Narrative

1. THE BEGINNING

"He's gone too," Jill, a dejected EMT, said. Both drivers were DOA leaving Jill with nothing to do but wait for the rest of the emergency crews too trickle in. It was 5:30 a.m on a rainy Tuesday morning, a morning beginning with death and judgment. As Jill walked away from the wreckage, towards the safety of her ambulance, she began to reflect on this most recent event.

It was an accident, Jill thought to herself. *It had to be.* Jill was no stranger to brutal car wrecks and while many could be faulted on an inebriated driver or reckless driving this accident could not. This accident was exactly that: an accident. The carnage at the scene pointed to a single scenario. Two cars hydroplaned on the small country road while traveling in opposite directions, one car coming from town, the other toward it. While trying to regain control they collided with each other in a metal crunching accident that rocketed both cars into the trees that lined the road. Centuries old behemoths created omnipotent poles that did not waiver as the cars wrapped themselves around their massive trunks like Christmas lights wrapped around a pine, their blinking tail lights created an eeire holiday setting at the appalling scene.

"God Dammit... Shit....This shit can't get any worse," yelled the sheriff, as he threw his hat into the mud in frustration.

"What is it Bill?" Jill responded. Spurred from her thoughts by his commotion.

The sheriff was at the blue pickup on the South side of the

road. Jill wasn't one for carnage and gore so once she declared the driver she left to check the other vehicle. The way the sheriff was acting Jill wondered if she had made a mistake.

"It's Mr. Witherspoon, Jill, this is his truck," the disgruntled sheriff answered as he pointed towards the license plate he clearly recognized. "He must have been on his way home from church. He sometimes stops there after his graveyard shift at the prison."

"Fuck," escaped Jill's lips as she absorbed Bill's information. *This does make this tragedy worse. Mr. Witherspoon, Mr. John Witherspoon, is beloved in our small town. He has a family of three and lives, and apparently dies, for the Lord. Raised from birth in this small town's church he has gone on more mission trips than anyone else, volunteers at local shelters, and left many promising job offers, from multiple accounting firms, to spread the good word to inmates as a janitor in the local prison. He was a rock in the community and his death could make....*

"SHIT!!!!! Jill you will never guess who the other victim is," Bill yelled out as he ran from his cruiser back to the other vehicle trying to confirm what he had just read on the screen.

Jolted from her thoughts Jill wondered what had the sheriff so excited. His voice was too giddy and happy considering this awful situation.

"It's that asshole Dr. Martin Andrews," Bill yelled to Jill, holding up a bloodied wallet as evidence. "He was that guest teacher, person, who attacked God last night. He was supposed to talk bout abortion, evolution, and that other crap today. Well, I guess God showed him who's boss. Just sucks that he had to send Mr. Witherspoon to do it."

With the wallet and a smug smile Bill began walking back to his cruiser to start his report. Walking across the slick pavement, towards her own vehicle, Jill struggled with the situation. With the facts coming into focus and the sound of sirens approaching Jill needed a minute to start to sort things out.

Dr. Andrews. Well, now the plot thickens, Jill thought as she took a seat on her back bumper. *While I don't agree with Bill's assessment of Dr. Andrews and his character I can understand the sentiment in this small town. This town revolves around the church, the university, and well the church. If pressed we could throw in the prison, but if nothing else this town lives for the Lord.*

Sitting on her back bumper Jill fumbled through her little med-kit, sorting it, before she left the scene.

I did not agree with everything Dr. Andrews said, but was intrigued and wanted to hear more. I was looking forward to his speech. Jill thought about a paper of his she had read as she closed up the back of her rig and walked towards the cockpit. *But in this town I am sure the smug look of Bill is just the beginning. Bill will do his best to vilify Dr. Andrews even though this accident was in no way his fault. Hell the entire town will vilify Dr. Andrews as they talk about acceptance and good will, qualities that oozed from Mr. Witherspoon.*

They will sanctify John as they burn Martin. In this town Dr. Andrews visit was equivalent to Satan himself rising from the ground. For a community so religious there is only one answer to what happened here.

Turning the key Jill adjusted her mirrors and took a look back at the scene. A circus of lights, fire rescue, and examiners enveloped the scene as they searched for answers to this awful accident.

The problem is... well I'm not sure they are wrong. What happened here was horrible. It was an accident. Yet I cannot shake the feeling that Bill is a little right. It hasn't rained in weeks and then tonight just enough fell to cause these drivers to lose control. Was this a simple accident or was there more? Was something divine going on here?

"I don't know why this happened, but I only hope that they felt nothing," Jill whispered to herself. Her swirling thoughts dissipated as she drove away from the scene.

Ready to let this go Jill was unaware that this drive, this awful morning, and her gut feeling were about to be the least of her problems. Jill was unaware that Pandora's box had just been opened in her life.

2. WELCOME TO THE END

A little woozy, Dr. Andrews woke on a cold, hard floor. Martin could not believe his eyes and was convinced he was delirious as he took in his surroundings.

He was sitting in a courthouse designed with the romanticized aesthetic of the Salem Witch Trials. Old benches formed the base of a gallery around and above him. They were divided from two sets of older chairs and tables by a simple half-wall. Everything faced the judge's podium which was adorned with a cross.

Time, Dr. Andrews thought, *will be my friend.* However, as he came out of his haze, the room did not disappear and Martin only became more confused. The last thing he remembered was losing control of his car in the rain. Now Dr. Andrews was sitting on the foggy floor of an antiquated courthouse. Martin could accept this as a coma or a dream, but it seemed so real. As the minutes passed Dr. Andrews lost faith in that idea.

I was driving. It was raining. There were lights and I lost control. Now... Now I'm in a luminescent, white marble, colonial courthouse. What is going on? This has to be a dream, or a coma... Dr, Andrews told himself despite his own feeling that this was much more. Struggling to regain his bearings Martin was too distracted to notice that he was not alone.

"I cannot believe that I am here," John, the room's other occupant, whispered under his breath. John was floating on cloud nine as he stood in middle of the courtroom and took it all in.

In front of John, past the benches, barrier, tables and podium shone the ever inviting pearly gates. He had waited his entire life to be here and now he stood on the doorstep to his Lord's kingdom.

Dropping to a knee John said a short prayer, thanking God for allowing him to be here and to be lucky enough to see the gates. John was thanking his Lord for letting him be a part of His greater plan and for anything that was about to come.

In his bliss Mr. Witherspoon had not noticed Dr. Andrews. John had noticed very little in the room outside of the pearly gate; however, there was one other thing that had caught his attention. Unable to stay content in his bliss Mr. Witherspoon could not battle his curiosity any longer.

Tearing his eyes away form the gate, John glanced over his shoulder and found a black obsidian door and what was intended to be a glance, turned into a deadly staring match for his soul. The door would not relinquish him. So dark and deep the door was and seemed to get richer and more sinister the longer he stared.

Trying to peel his eyes back to the Gate of God John searched the door for something that would break the black and relinquish his gaze. The door had no handle, window, or decoration. It was solid and reeked of sin. Panicked John now knew how Eve felt and could not break away from this forbidden fruit. He was frustrated and angry with himself. John had always avoided sin, and now, in the house of God, he was transfixed by the only thing that did not share his light.

Bewitched by sin, John was losing all hope when he heard a small cough. Like the voice of an angel, John listened for another and when it came he was able to break away. Searching for the source John found Dr. Andrews doubled over on the floor trying to regain his bearings.

"You okay?" John asked Martin as he shuffled through the benches towards his new friend.

Startled by John's voice Dr. Andrews lost his balance and fell onto the cold, luminescent, marble floor.

"Oh, sorry," John said as he reached for his new friend. "I didn't mean to startle you. I just wanted to make sure you are okay. I am in your debt, friend, and owe you my gratitude though. I was so focused on that black door I could not pull myself away. I did not know how to get back here and then your cough broke the hold that sinful, door held on me…"

Dr. Andrews only caught the first few words and lost the rest after John said "that black door." Dr. Andrews was aware that his new companion was still talking, but could not focus on him as he took in the door. Dr. Andrews inspected it for a minute. The dark obsidian seemed so out of place; however, if you saw it for what it was, as a break in the white, then it opened one's eyes to the beauty that truly surrounded him.

Around the door Martin was able to see that the white walls were not only luminescent, but also intricately carved. What he once thought was flat marble was in fact decorated with vivid scenes depicting folklore and religions from all of history. One scene depicted the story of Cain and Able, while a few millimeters away the Egyptian God Osiris rode across the sky. Above the door were primitive cave paintings to gods Martin did not even know, which were right below the most magnificent depictions of Athena and Zeus. The images and stories melded and mixed together into a symphony of visual chaos that touched every wall, bench, chair, and podium. Every surface in the room was a piece of art.

"..... I just cannot believe that we are here I mean...." John rambled on. His hand absentmindedly extended to Martin in a gesture of assistance and friendship.

"If you don't mind me asking: Where are we and who exactly are you?" Dr. Andrews interrupted John's unwavering dialogue as he finally took John's hand.

"Sorry, I must have forgotten to introduce myself," John responded as they shook hands after Martin finally stood up. "Well I am John Witherspoon, but you can call me John. As for where we are, do you really need to ask? I mean we are here. We made it to the gates of the Lord and if you don't mind me asking who am I spending this blessed time with?"

"Oh, I'm Dr. Martin Andrews, but please just call me Martin.... Sorry about my confusion I'm still in shock. This is the last place I ever thought that I would be today..."

"I know the feeling," John nodded in agreement.

For the next few minutes Martin and John exchanged small talk. Somehow talking to and around each other at the same time. Both of them were in shock, but neither one of them seemed to see what the other did. John saw the place of his Lord, while Martin saw a temple to many faiths.

Martin spent his mental energy trying to figure out if this place was real while John bathed in the bliss of his faith as he took in the Kingdom of his Lord. He filled their conversation by pointing out his favorite bible stories on the decorated walls, somehow missing the stories Martin pointed out surrounding them.

During this time together they both failed to notice the third party that had entered the luminescent chamber. Their judge had arrived and was ready to begin.

3. THE BOTTOMLESS WELL

The door to Bottomless Well creaked as Jill walked in. The Bottomless Well was like any other, dimly lit, run down, small town dive bar. The profits from the local drunks were just enough to keep the place afloat and illegal activity was as popular as the tap and supplemented the owner quite well. 80's rock enhanced the broken bar stools, worn pool tables, and dirty booths. If you had cash no questions were asked. Your business was your own and it was bar policy to keep it that way.

Walking up to the bar Jill slapped a 20 down while asking for a double shot of Jack. Downing the shot Jill told the ancient barman and owner to keep them coming, wishing he would just leave the bottle, as she took her stool at the bar. From her perch Jill took in her surroundings with a second shot. She had not been to this den of despair since her undergraduate days and, like everything else in this small town, it had not changed at all.

The same bar stools were broken, the same fans lazily spun with time being shown by an additional layer of dust. Jill laughed to herself after spotting old Jim the local pool shark. A group of young "thugs" who thought they owned the world had challenged Jim and Jill knew that in 20 minutes or so they would be sulking out of this dingy bar with their tails between their legs; their billfolds considerably lighter.

Like old Jim the rest of the hookers and hustlers were the same ones Jill had seen years earlier and continued to make their rounds. Local drunks wailed their worries to anyone who would listen, while other patrons would disappear form time to time engage in their own business. Some got quickies in the bathroom or parking lot, while others placed bets or picked up their "meds". The "bouncer" was the same off-duty cop who had served this joint for as long as anyone could remember. Ripe with corruption he became blind to anything if you slipped him the right dead president.

That bouncer was one of the reasons Jill and her friends had fallen in love with this place. When they were younger Andrew Jackson got them in the door and from there they had their own personal Vegas. They could drink, smoke, shoot pool or be with whoever they wanted. The world was their oyster and they were free to explore it. Young and stupid they thought this place was the best place to spread their wings of maturity, adulthood, and freedom. They were too young and oblivious to understand that this "bar" was no more than a prison of pain and despair.

Raising her glass to take another sip Jill found it, just like everything else in her life, empty. Turing back to the bar her glass made a little chink as as she waited for her next dose of numbness. Waiting patiently Jill reminisced on the disaster day that brought her here for her self-prescribed medication.

I still can't believe this shit... First the crash... than Jeff... Then the paper work... and ahh!!! Just FUCK IT ALL!!!!! Jill's thoughts screamed in her head as she tried to make sense of it all.

After the early crash had been cleared Jill received an

emergency call from her fiancé Jeff. He was a Marine who had just come home from a two year deployment. Less than a week into his return, just when Jill thought that he was back, his unit was recalled for emergency deployment. There was no warning, no time, all she received was a 30 second call from Jeff telling her that he was being deployed, he loved her, and he would call her when he could. It happened so fast Jill did not have an opportunity to say a word before Jeff had hung up, let alone make it home to say goodbye.

Reeling from the crash and Jeff's deployment Jill got a call from a co-worker whose kid was sick, hoping Jill could cover her shift. Grateful for the distraction Jill accepted the extra shift. After a second twelve hour shift, Jill was ready for the nightmare day to end when things got exponentially worse.

"Mr. Crasnick, I understand you wanted to see me?" Jill said in a hushed nervous tone as she entered the sterile office of the Dean of Medicine. Being summoned after her long day.

"Yes yes, come in Mrs. Harris, is it?" Mr. Crasnick, the large man behind the desk responded as he invited her to a seat across from him.

"It has come to our attention that a grave misfortune happened regarding your 5:30 call and the media." Jill's heart sank as she wondered what possibly could happen to make this day's events even worse. "You see there was a *leak insinuating that this crash was caused by some sort of religious zealot attacking the sinner Dr. Andrews in a jihadist manner. This is not only an egregious allegation against one of this towns great people, Mr. Witherspoon, but is also slanderous towards the church and all our town holds dear. Beyond this, there are reports of incompetence on the part of our hospital raising questions about the care we gave the victims. Some are reporting that these two men could have been saved. As an organization, a place of care, we cannot stand for this type of behavior and we cannot let one bad apple spoil the whole bushel. Once you have found the leak you have to fix it. Don't you agree Mrs. Harris."*

Sitting mute Jill was stunned as she listened to Mr. Crasnick lecture her knowing what was coming next. She was being blamed for this "leak" and any of the repercussions associated with it. She was Mr. Carasnick's sacrificial lamb and even though she wanted to respond she knew nothing would change his mind and could only make matters worse. Jill knew that she would find herself alone at home in the foreseeable future. The only question that remained was for how long and if she was suspended or fired.

"As you understand Mrs. Harris we take these allegations very seriously and cannot condone this behavior. I also saw that you took an extra 12 hour shift today, something that is against company policy without direct approval. This violation along with allegations that you did not do your job this morning, while they do not reflect your work history with us, Mrs. Harris we cannot over look them. As you know when we took you on we overlooked some indiscretions on your college transcript and police record. This incident has made us revisit those cases and have

raised questions about your character. Because of the severity of this incident, the leak, and the possibility of inadequate care or malfeasance on the part of this hospital we have to investigate what happened today. Until we know the extent of your involvement you are suspended without pay."

Jill's mind had run blank from there. Jill did not recall anything about how she left the hospital or how she got to this bar. All Jill knew was now she at this shitty bar, reminiscing about her awful day, ready to drink the night away.

With a full glass Jill turned away from the bar and reflected on everything that Mr. Crasnick had used to justify her suspension. The idea that taking an extra shift was a justification was laughable. While "technically" against company policy, taking an extra shift was actively encouraged when the hospital was short staffed, which was a chronic, cost saving condition. Inadequate treatment, or whatever he called it, was also impossible because the bodies were mangled in the carnage of steel and nature. Mercifully both of them were DOA, if they hadn't been there would have been no way to extract them before they died a slow and painful death. Jill was not the leaker, she knew that, but Mr. Crasnick needed a scapegoat and when it came down to it the indiscretions in her past were all he really needed to scapegoat her. It was a single incident that ironically had started on the same stool she sat on now.

The incident had started innocently enough, Jill was young and having fun. She had a few drinks and the guy sitting next to her doing his best to talk his way into her pants. Jill was not interested and despite her protests the guy never stopped his futile attempts to put the moves on her. As the night wore on he got more adventurous and she slapped him after his hand had started exploring her thigh underneath her skirt. Unfortunately for Jill she did not know how this bar worked at the time and the gentleman, treating her like a piece of meat, was a good friend of the bouncer and an officer of the law.

Seconds after she slapped the guy the bouncer was whipping out cuffs as the "victim" screamed assault. In a rush of emotion Jill yelled that she wanted the pig charged with sexual assault and, in the end, that was her downfall. Her outburst caused a commotion and landed her outside in the back of the "victim's" squad car with his partner, an on duty cop, filling out paper work. For years Jill wondered if things would have been different if she had just stayed calm. She was told she thrown out because she acted up, because the bartender did not want to "disturb his other guests."

Nineteen and in the back of a squad car Jill watched the charges pile up. What started out as disturbing the peace morphed into assaulting an officer and resisting arrest. It took the cops a few minutes to find Jill's two ID's and that is when things went from bad to worse. Underage and scared Jill was being lectured by two dirty cops throwing around terms like "felony" and "finished". Jill did not know her rights and with years in jail appearing before her she said something she would regret. Jill told the officers that: "she would do anything if they would drop the charges and forget this ever happened."

After an hour of "unique compensation" Jill was used and abused in the back of the car with additional charges of bribery and prostitution. The cops let her stew during their a celebratory drink and cigarette before dropping all but a disturbing the peace charge. After some community service Jill was free to go on with her life. Her record blackened forever despite her work as a street walker.

That night was the last time Jill had been to any bar alone. She went to a few others with friends once or twice for a bachelorette party here and there, but she never dreamed of going to a bar alone again. Let alone this one.

Things change though and after the day Jill had day even the Devil would pity her. She did not care that she had been raped here. Jill needed a distraction and a place where she could be alone.

I can't believe this shit.... I mean..... Jill's thoughts raced as she downed another double shot.

Slamming her glass Jill took stock of the bar. Jim had freed the "punks" of their discretionary allowance. The kids were nowhere to be seen and had probably already run home. In a dimly lit corner one of the Bottomless Well's more "gifted" girls was giving a quick demonstration of her talents to an older patron, giving him a taste of what he could have for a minimal investment.

At the next table an awkward first date was stalling for the third time as their neighbor's moans filled the lulls of their conversation. Down the bar from her Jill watched two guys trying to convince a titillating blonde bombshell that they could give her the best night of her life.

Raising her glass to parched lips Jill chuckled to herself. "It never ceases to amaze me how far guys will go for a little tail. They think they are better than that old man in the back booth, but, in reality, they are probably worse."

Tilting the glass back Jill waited for the sweet elixir to find her throat, but nothing came. Holding the glass in front of her Jill examined it trying to understand why her lips were dry and why the glass was empty.

"Hey barkeep!" Jill yelled with a raised glass. Frustrated she was being pulled away from the drama unfolding around her.

"You get more once I have your keys," the bartender barked at Jill in his gruff tone. "And don't get prissy with me," he continued as Jill started to act up. "You can drink yourself unconscious for all I care. Just, if you want any more, then you ain't driving out of here tonight young lady."

Perturbed Jill fumbled for her keys and handed them over. In return the bartender refilled Jill's double and gave her another on the house. Thankful for his generosity it took a single sip for Jill to become less perturbed by his demand and more grateful for it. She was in no state to drive and Jill knew the night was still very young, these drinks were just the tip of the iceberg. Jill was ready to forget the day and, taking a sip, she was starting to think that someone was finally looking out for her.

4. FIRST IMPRESSIONS

"Yep... I mean... I just can't believe it!!!!" John said in an exuberant shout. His joy still overflowing from his excitement to entering the kingdom.

"Yeah, it's great," Martin replied politely, continually looking around in disbelief and confusion.

Martin agreed with John it certainly did look like they were at the gates of heaven. It was less fluffy clouds and more courtroom, but there was no denying what the place, and gate, identified as. However, Martin could not make sense of all the other religious iconography present. Mandalas, Greek Gods, Islamic, and Jewish art were just a few of the countless faiths interwoven into a background of beauty lining every surface of this place.

Despite the beauty and iconography Martin wondered: *Why were the gates of heaven in a courtroom? What did they need to do to enter the gates? If they were at the Kingdom of God why were they they only ones here? Surely they were not the only people who died yesterday.*

Determined to not think about his troubling thoughts Martin turned his attention to the one thing he had not examined: The Gate.

Convinced his eyes were playing tricks on him Martin blinked and squinted as he tried to figure out what was standing just behind the judge's bench, in front of the gate. The being appeared to have a white robe, was slender, with long hair and a full beard. If someone asked Martin would say he was Jesus; however, Martin could not be sure. Martin was forced to shield his eyes because, somehow, the being was emanating more light than the luminous courtroom around him.

Martin blinked and could not believe his eyes. The beard was gone. So was the hair and slender frame. The robe was now a dirt orange and what started out as Jesus transformed into what he would identify as Buddha. Before Martin could process the new identity the being changed into Moses, then Thor, Zeus, Mars, Athena, and Osiris. Whatever stood in front of him was too bright and changing too fast for Dr. Andrews to identify.

The lack of response alerted John to the fact that Martin was no longer listening to his jubilant prattle. Following Martin's eyes John turned his head, lost his breath, and became transfixed by the same thing Martin had.

John could not believe his eyes, behind the judge's bench stood John's savior and Lord. With white robes and a kind smile John took in all of his Lord's features. His broad shoulders, long hair, and gentle eyes, full of understanding and compassion.

"Oh.. my..." John released an audible whisper, blissfully aware of his good fortune. He could barely believe that he was in the presence of his Lord.

John averted his gaze as he began to tear up. He had lived his entire life for this one moment, all the sacrifice and challenges had led up to this one moment and now, in the presence of his Lord, John knew that it had all been worth it. John had lived right. He had followed his path. More than anything an all encompassing safety overwhelmed John as a feeling of peace. John knew that he would be okay now and for all eternity.

"My two friends please do not be scared or overwhelmed;

you are safe here. You are in a place where we will have plenty of time to talk and get to know each other."

Looking back at the Entity Martin was frozen, lost for words, and unsure what to do. His instincts told him to run, but that was not really an option. Instead he just stood, stared, and listened as John knelt in humbled bliss.

"Please, my friends, I know this is confusing, but we have plenty of time to talk, explore, and understand. Please get off of the cold floor and join me in the front of the court." The Entity invited them forward by pointing to two tables just beyond the barrier that separated the court from the gallery.

Without any other options Dr. Andrews walked to the front of the court as the Entity was transforming into Estsanatlehi. Entering the front of the court, Dr. Andrews felt like he was in a crime drama. The two tables faced the grand judge's desk, which had two smaller desk flanking it across the length of the wall in front of the gate. There was no space for a jury and the gallery stood behind him seeming a mile away now. Taking a chance Martin cautiously sat behind the table to his left, at the defendants station, waiting for whatever was about to come. Painfully aware of what the Entity had called this place.

Mr. Witherspoon took his time to get to the front of the courtroom as he took in the beauty of the room. His favorite stories: Cain and Able, David and Goliath, and the reseurection, seemed to jump out of the walls around him and whenever he felt like it was too much he could literally look to his Lord.

Once John reached the barrier he took a deep breath before stepping into the same space as his Lord. John couldn't help but stare in wonderment at the large cross which adorned the Lords grand bench and following it to its completion he found his Lord offering him a seat at the table opposite Martin. Unlike his friend John moved without hesitation to the prosecutors station.

"Thank you Lord," John thanked his Lord as he took his seat.

"Now that you are seated up here please do not be afraid or scared. The only trial here is one of speech. You will not need to battle hordes of villains or do other feats of strength to demonstrate your faith. All that awaits you now is a conversation to see if you are ready to enter the eternal bliss. "

The Entity's invitation seemed so simple that fear settled a little deeper into Martin's soul. *John is so confident that Jesus is standing before us and I just don't know,* Martin thought to himself as he assessed the situation. *If this is indeed heaven why are there so many religious symbols? Why is the podium littered with things from many faiths?* True to form where John saw a cross, Martian saw a symbol that integrated symbology from a variety of faiths.

"If you agree to participate we will talk about everything. I want to know about your lives, your beliefs, and anything else that comes to mind. I want your input on a series of events unfolding on Earth. I want your opinions, ideas, and what you think should be done. Once we have talked, and hopefully come to a consensus, we will know who is ready. This is about your story and it is important to remember that you two are not fighting against each other. There is no shame in not participating."

With his invitation given the eternal Entity took a moment to observe his guests. As expected John was overcome with bliss. His faith had conditioned him for this moment with years of perparation and anticipation. On the other hand Martin was confused and overwhelmed. His own curiosity and doubt had him questioning the complexity of everything he had ever know. Chuckling to itself the Entity was amused and couldn't help but think of how amazing the mind is. People see what they want to see even in the presence of facts and knowledge to the contrary.

"My Lord, I would be honored to speak with you," John

spoke almost as soon as the Entity had finished. The Entity nodded and the court turned to Martin.

Martin was quiet, confused, and his senses were a mess. Martin wanted answers and knowledge, but he did not know if he could find them here. He did not trust his eyes, ears, or nose. He didn't trust anything he felt and the last thing Martin needed was a metaphysical discussion about the meaning of life.

Sitting there, even with the eyes of the court on him, Martin somehow knew he could take as long as he wanted to answer. John and the Entity would never force an answer from him and that peace gave Martin something to trust: Time. He may not be able to trust any of his senses; however, he knew, in this place, that time was on his side.

"I agree with John. Let's begin."

5. OPENING STATEMENTS

"To begin, I would like each of you to introduce yourselves as if we had never met. Imagine we had just met on the street or at a cafe," the Entity said as he cast his gaze towards John.

"Hi, my name is John Witherspoon," John started with a jump. "I'm a proud Baptist, have two lovely girls and a loving wife. I have done everything in your name," John concluded unintentionally, still working out the jitters of speaking to his savior.

Waiting for some type of response John stared at the Entity and saw the smile of his savior cast back at him. Martin, also staring, saw the intimidating eyes of Zeus mulling over John's response.

Without a single word the Entity gave John a nod and shifted his focus to Dr. Andrews.

"Hello, my name is Dr. Martin Andrews. I am a professor and comparative religions scholar. I have dedicated my life to studying religions, faiths, and belifes stemming from the farthest reaches of our globe throughout time. After years of study I have become agnostic…" Martin's strong introduction quickly trailed off. Averting his gaze Dr. Andrews felt stupid, he never introduced him self as an agnostic, let alone in this place.

"Well, it is nice to meet you both," The Entity started. "A little formal for a coffee shop, but now that we know where everyone is coming from I would like to get a better sense of how you identify your religious beliefs. I understand that you told me what you are, but now I would like to know why. What brought you to your beliefs and faith?" The Entity paused as it looked across the highly decorated courtroom, and back to its two friends. "Dr. Andrews, why don't you start. I am very curious how you came to find your beliefs. Start wherever you want and take your time. If you need any refreshment or food, ask and it shall be provided. No alcoholic requests yet. It is early and I want both of you to be as mentally awake and able as possible."

Looking away from Moses, Martin found the marble floor, closed his eyes, relaxed his mind, and came to three thoughts: First, a stiff drink sounded amazing. Second, when did God's start making jokes? And third where did he start?

Did he start with his childhood? Or when his religious journey started? Did he talk about how he came into his profession or why he was an atheist?

Opening his eyes Martin saw the scene of Athenas birth staring back at him from the marble floor. That scene faded into the story of Judas, which was right underneath a traditional Cherokee creation story. These three scenes and the ones that flowed around them gave Martin a place to start.

"Growing up I always loved stories. I just loved them. My first memory is of my Grandfather reading to me. Stories were and have always been what grounds me.

"I was brought up in a mixed household. My Father was Christian, my mother Jewish, and while it was not perfect, love seemed to transcend any religious barriers. Because of their faiths I was brought up hearing the stories and doctrines of each faith. At thirteen I was given my Bar Mitzvah, and all in all I did my best to try and follow both faiths as best I could.

"Unfortunately my desire to please both parents and faiths was doomed from the start. I was always the most vocal in my youth groups because of my struggle to follow both faiths. The Rabis and Minsters started out nice by giving me answers like "all God cares about is that you are a good person," or "God knows what is in our heart." As I got older the nice answers became harsher and I was told that I could not marry the two faiths. I was confused, lost, and as I entered high-school I began to doubt myself and my faith.

"I attended services throughout high-school, however in college everything changed. I continued to struggle until my history 101 class when I learned all about the faith, or as my teachers called them "myths", of the Greeks and Egyptians. I was enamored with the stories and iconography so much that I sought out the religious studies department to learn more. In the beginning I think I did it hoping I could find a way to marry my faiths, but before long I was studying every faith I could find; attending as many services, practices, and rituals that I could.

"I changed my degree and before long my undergraduate studies were complete. In graduate school I realized that, despite years of trying, I couldn't marry my two different faiths. More importantly I couldn't logically follow one faith over another. I had been introduced to so many different ways of explaining the universe that I could not justify placing faith in one above another. From everything that I had learned I felt that every society could not be wrong, but at the same time I wondered how could they all be right with such different answers. Where did science fit into this equation? Each day more questions appeared as I searched for the truth. I dedicated my life to research in an effort to help combat the hate and conflict propagated by different religious beliefs. My inability to pick one religion is why I am agnostic. I search for truth and common ground that I hope would help me find answers and faith that I long for."

Sitting down Martin finished his declaration and wanted to know if it had made any sense. He felt like he had been mumbling the entire time and wondered if his answer was right? Should he have claimed he was Jewish? Was Baptist the right answer? Was there a right answer?

Martin looked back to the Entity to find Athena staring down at him, wearing, what he swore, was a slight smile before she spoke.

"Very insightful and interesting Dr. Andrews. What about you Mr. Witherspoon? How did you come to your faith?"

Still engaged with Dr. Andrews's story, his Lord's question caught John off guard. Looking away from Dr. Andrews to the smiling face of the Son lifted him to speak.

"Well my Lord…

6. THE WAKING NIGHTMARE

Jill woke up with her head pounding of jack and little sleep; wearing nothing but a sleep shirt.

"How the hell did I get here?" Jill wondered as she began to sit up in her empty bed.

Looking around Jill was in the same room with the same dresser and the same shabby, particle board, bookcase. Devoid of much personality or trinkets, this was her bedroom and normally she didn't mind the shabbiness; however, with her fiancé's spot empty it was all a little sad.

Jill let her feet fall to the floor, bracing herself on her arms, and stretching out her neck and back, Jill was determined to get up and moving. Ready to wash away the smell of pain, defeat, and loneliness.

Making her way to the bathroom Jill found her clothes scattered about the room. In general disbelief Jill wondered what had possibly gotten into her last night. She was never a messy person, she prided herself on that fact, but apparently last night the hamper was too far away for her to reach. Kicking the clothes out of the way Jill finished her trek to the bathroom ready to wash the nightmare away.

Starting the shower Jill felt dirty, cheap, and was ready to get back to normal. However, the state of the bedroom and a general feeling of dread worried Jill. She wanted to chalk it up to the night of drinking, but her gut told her different, this was something the hot water was not washing away.

Basking in the steam of the shower Jill told herself the feeling was because of the drinks and that "normal" was different now. Her fiancé was gone and she was unemployed. Jill told herself this over and over again, but could not shake the weight on her chest away. She knew that something else was wrong. Something was off. Still in denial Jill reached for her shampoo, but grabbed her husband's instead.

"Who moved my shit?" Jill said to herself as she searched for her shampoo, eventually finding it resting on the shower floor.

Lathering her hair Jill tried to relax, if she didn't she would drive herself insane. No one was out to get her and no one had been in her house let alone her bathroom. If anything she had knocked the shampoo over in a drunken stupor. It was nothing, no harm no foul, she was as safe now as she had been last night.

Getting out of the shower Jill reached for her towel, but couldn't find it. She continued to fight this internal struggle as thoughts crept back into her mind about intruders, but after a deep breath she put them to rest. Her towel was on the other bar, and while drying off Jill looked around her bathroom and didn't find anything else devious or malicious. Her tooth brush was still wet, her shampoo had fallen and her towel was in a different place, but beyond that her bathroom was the same as it always was. It was not the disaster that her bedroom had been, but it all could be explained by a bad night of drinking.

"Shit," she said as she put her scrubs away. "I guess I won't need these for a while," Jill whispered to herself as she found more casual clothes to wear for the day.

Jill finished getting dressed and decided to explore her

empty home. Going room to room Jill was a little surprised to find everything in order. There was a glass out of place in the living room and a rug was askew, but nothing was really out of the normal.

Jill went through the house twice and although everything seemed fine something was haunting her. Jill searched a third and fourth time looking for something to prove her paranoia.

The clock showed 1 p.m. by the time Jill decided everything was safe. Without a job to go to Jill decided the best use of her time would be to piece her night together, hoping that it would put the feeling in her gut to rest.

With a decision made, Jill gathered her purse and walked out the door. Locking up the house Jill was ready to call a cab when she saw something that forced her to drop everything.

Her car was sitting in front of her apartment.

Fear raced through Jill. Now she knew something was wrong. She didn't remember much from the night before but she remembered the bartender taking her keys. Considering her pounding headache there was no way that he would have let her drive home. The man had his flaws, but he was not going to jail because of her.

What do I do? Do I call the police, a girl friend, my fiancé? Jill thought to herself.

Jill knew what she wanted to do. She wanted to call her fiancé; however, if that was an option she probably wouldn't be in this position to begin with.

Taking a deep breath Jill gathered herself and jumped in her car. It was time for answers and the bar was the best place to start.

7. A TOAST TO
THE TRUTH

The bar was fairly empty, but pretty much the same from the night before. An off duty cop still manned the door demanding his fee from any patron who walked in. In the daylight Jill could see that the bar was still the deplorable mess she remembered with a layer of grime and dust covering everything. A few business men were taking an extended happy hour and absent a night walker it looked like the time of day did not change what this place was.

Jill sat down at the same spot she did the night before and waited for the barman to acknowledge her. The man saw her, it was the same man from the night before, but he refused to come closer. Jill waited patiently for over a half an hour as the barman did everything he could think of to avoid approaching her. He pretended to dust, pretended to take inventory, and pretended to wash some glassware. His eyes continually darting back to see if Jill had disappeared.

Jill wanted to be angry, but could hardly imagine she was the first midday visit this man had ever received and understood how they must normally go. This time of day the patrons were either a local drunk, a local hot shot, looking to celebrate a good morning, or an angry patron from the night before. Jill fell into that last category so she could hardly blame the man for avoiding her.

Once the barman had exhausted the amount of glasses he

could polish or counter space he could wipe down, he approached Jill on the offensive.

"Look young lady you're not getting any right now. You had a lot last night and you can do better," the barman told Jill as he joined her.

Cute, Jill thought to herself. *Apparently I found the only chivalrous bartender in town. Good thing I have business and am not here to drink.*

"I didn't come to drink, I came to ask about last-"

Before Jill could finish the bartender cut her off.

"-Look little missy whatever you did last night I am not liable for. So if you think you can pin any of your shit on me you have got another thing coming."

Even though Jill thought she had prepared herself, his hostile tone still shocked Jill. However, after a moment of reflection, Jill reminded herself that she was not the first nor would she be the last to ask him this question. The midday bar crowd brought him nothing but trouble.

"It's nothing like that," Jill said as the bartender started to turn away. "I don't think you are responsible for anything. I just need to know what happened to me last night. The last thing I remember was handing you my keys. I was hoping you could help me fill in the blanks." Jill finished her plea as he began to polish another hopeless cause.

His old rag going between the glass and his shoulder the man looked over Jill a few times trying to decide if she was worth the trouble. After an eternity of silence the bartender deemed Jill worthy of his time and started to speak.

"First, you need to be clear that I'm not responsible for anything that happened last night.' Jill nodded in agreement as the bartender recited his conditions. 'And second, I don't want you talking bad about me because of what went down. This has always been a place for all types and I can't have people who make a mistake ruining it for everyone."

Jill nodded wondering what she could possibly say that would hurt this places reputation.

"Well, alright then. I can tell you what happened to you last night, cause of the ruckus you caused. I mean with the hell you gave that friend of yours, I'm surprised you let him bring you home."

Jill's mind began to race wondering what the bartender was talking about. She was a docile, peaceful drunk, unless she was provoked. What had possibly happened last night and, considering this bar's patrons, who would she have possibly let give her a ride home?

The bartender waited as Jill processed the information.

"And you wouldn't happen to remember that friends name would you?" Jill asked.

"Yeah... You yelled it enough times. Greg something and his friend. um... eh..."

"Drew," Jill finished his sentence as the memory from last night started to flood back.

"You can get more once I have your keys...You can keep drinking, hell I don't care if you drink your weight in whisky, you just aren't driving out of here tonight young lady"

After handing him her keys Jill waited as the bartender poured her another double, this one was on the house the

33

bartender told her.

"This night is getting a little better," Jill thought as she enjoyed her drink. That thought did not last long though as Jill heard an all too familiar voice yelling out for her behind her.

"Jill, girl...Jill... hey turn around... I know you can hear me."

Turning Jill's fears were confirmed as the last person she wanted to see walked towards her.

"Jill, I'd like you to meet my friend Andrew, Andrew this is Jill. Andrew is on leave. His unit just got back last week," Greg finished the introductions.

"You can call me Drew," the young man said extending his hand.

Ignoring Greg, Jill focused on Andrew and asked "22nd division right?" Jill asked him making a point to shake his hand to show her disdain for Greg.

"Yeah... thats right, but how..."

"Man, she just knows and has a thing for army guys. I've been trying to get her attention for years now, but she will just not budge," Greg interrupted before Jill could answer.

Piercing Greg with a glance Jill did not even want to dignify his statement with a response. Greg was a pig, jackass, jerk, prick, spoiled, and above all else the Dean of medicines god damn son. Ever since she arrived in this town Greg had been infatuated with her. She tried to be polite, but he would not stop, not even after she got married. Of course since then his tactics had changed. Instead of just stalking her, Greg took it upon himself to make her life a living hell. He was a fucking six year old who picks on the girl he likes. All of this was irrelevant right now and turning to Andrew, Jill decided that he didn't deserve to be condemned based on association.

"Sorry bout Greg, Drew. I recognized you from your graduation, you were in the same training class as my husband. He's in unit 25."

"Oh… well that makes sense and I'm sorry about his deployment. His troop actually saved mine from that deployment," Andrew responded with compassion Jill would not have expected from one of Greg's friends.

With introductions complete Greg and Andrew took up residence around Jill. It would not have been too bad if Greg wasn't there, but because he was Jill now knew how the blonde at the end of the bar felt. In the back of Jill's mind she wondered if the blonde had any ideas on how to get away from a situation like this.

"So Jill you are home alone then?" Greg asked as he began sipping his drink.

Flashing her ring Jill responded. "Nope still got my cat." It was a lie, she couldn't have a pet, but she would say anything that could stop Greg in his tracks.

"Ah come on, don't you want some companionship. I mean I'm sure Andrew wouldn't mind if we bailed on him, unless he wants to come along?" Greg continued his approach as he physically moved closer.

Andrew shifted uncomfortably. He did not want to insult his friend, but obviously did not want to support him in any way. This did not go unnoticed by Jill who was thankful she was not the only one disgusted with Greg.

"Umm… Greg how about not. Not only am I saying no, but if you keep up like this, this will be my last drink before you watch me leave," Jill answered as sternly and clearly as possible as she picked up and consumed a little more of her drink.

"No need for that. No need. It was just a joke. We are all friends here. Come on Jill let me get you another round or two," Greg retreated, trying to make sure Jill did not leave.

Another round was poured and Jill remembered very little of the conversation they exchanged from there.

Jill looked up from her flashback searching for the barkeep. Calling him over Jill wondered what else happened after her memory had dissolved back into reality.

"Sorry about this, but do you remember what happened after Greg ordered the round?" Jill asked trying to fill in the missing blanks.

"Yeah, you drank that round and then another two with them. You yelled at him every time he made a move. Then you disappeared into the bathroom for a little bit. When you reappeared you pretty much left."

Her mind wandered. The barkeep had jogged her memory a little. She remembered going to the bathroom, but nothing after that. Getting up from the creaking barstool Jill walked towards the cesspools called bathrooms hoping something there would jog her memory.

8. GRACE

"I was just a few days old the first time I attended one of your glorious services," Mr. Witherspoon started. His Lord and savor staring down at him from his perch before the pearly gates.

"Of course, I don't really remember it, but I have been basking in your love and glory for my entire life. At six months I was baptized and again at nine and 31. I have attended bible study and church every Tuesday, Wednesday, Thursday, and Sunday well for as long as I can remember.

"Yes sir, I have been blessed to be in your light and glory my entire life. Following your good word as the truth, I have let it guide me through many tough situations. When I strayed you always caught me. When I faltered you found me. You never left, but were always there with open arms and love. You guided me away from a life of corruption and sin offered by the secular accounting firms that wanted me and guided me into a janitorial position that brought me more fulfillment than I ever would have imagined. I know I did not always agree with your plan, but I always had faith that my life would be blessed if I lived it in your glory and put my trust in your hands."

Mr. Witherspoon finished his speech beaming with pride. It was more eloquent than he thought it would be, but he chalked that up to being in his Lord's presence. Not peeling his eyes away from the son the deity gave him a once over before asking John a question.

"Is that all you have to say? These are the reasons you came to the church?"

Mr. Witherspoon's smile faltered because he did not know how to answer. He had struggled to find the right words and apparently he had not said enough. His story had been much more than Sunday school and blessed givings. He had struggled, he fought, and at times he had hated his faith and his Lord.

Looking back to his God, John could not believe that he would gloss over so much of his life and what really brought then together. His Lord was sitting in front of him right now. He was giving him a chance to express his faith and tell his story and John gave a cliff notes version, a half tale, a truth that no one would want to listen to. Taking a deep breath John felt a twinge of fear as he began to bare his full heart and story.

"Well, no sir, there is much more that brought me to you," John nervously continued. Waiting for a sign Jesus gave him a slight nod and John continued.

"You see, I struggled. Like anyone else I struggled to live a good life. But it was your word and guidance, it came to me in so many ways and in so many blessings that kept me going. It changed my life and was so clear I could not help but believe and follow you."

Pausing for a second John looked back up at his Lord. Again he gave him a nod of approval that helped propel John.

"You put me in a home, that while very loving and devoted, also tested me. I remember my father would read the bible to me and my siblings every night when I was young. He would quiz us on how well we knew the stories and how well we listened. I did my best to learn, but sometimes it wasn't enough for him. Now I know that his behavior was part of a test of my own faith and patience.

"As you know Lord, well, my father drank. And when he drank

he became abusive. It was not his fault, but he was not strong enough to avoid or overcome the Devil's liquid," John continued as tears fell to the pure marble floor. "He would beat me and my sisters. Once he even raped them and I hated you for it. My father would quote the same passages he read us the night before as justification for his actions. But now, right now, my gut feeling is confirmed. His actions were a test of faith, to see if I could see through what he was doing and if I could follow your lessons and glory."

The new revelations about John's life took Martin by surprise. He would have never expected such horrors to dot his past; however, he could not help but wonder why he thought it was a test? Why he did not do more to get himself and his siblings the help they desperately needed.

"You wanted me to honor my mother and father. You wanted me to show the compassion Jesus did. You wanted me to do my best for my father, while helping the rest of my family. You wanted me to help my father through his sin and back to you. To find salvation once again. It was hard. It was hard to know that you had a plan for us and for me, but in time your plan and glory became clear. You showed me the truth in your words even when people used it for their own devious means.

"Because of my belief, my faith, and my prayers, you helped and you answered. You sent the counselor to become our new neighbor. You sent him as an answer, a gift, to my prayers. He not only helped lead my father away from the bottle, but he also helped my sisters and I see your greater plan. Lord I thank you now again, like I did back then, for all of your patience and guidance with me. It was the day you sent Jeremy into our life that I knew I could trust you. It was that day that I truly realized your grace and love. That it would never sour or tarnish and that you would always be there."

Looking up through his tear stricken eyes John felt a sense of joy and bliss he had never felt before. Here he was spilling his heart to the one he loved most. He was getting the opportunity to show God why he loved and followed him so. John was at the gates of glory talking to his creator. He was getting a chance to directly express his love and thanks.

"After that day Lord, as you know, I rededicated myself to you. Starting in the seventh grade I spent my summers on mission trips. I went around the world bringing your good word and love to all I met. I volunteered at the prison for many years, delivering food and the good word to the inmates at their meal time. In high school I volunteered at the homeless shelter and started a bible study group to bring understanding, love, and glory to your name.

"I chose my college because it was devoid of your grace. I chose them so I could bring your light and grace to them. And after four years of study the school that had been devoid of your grace had a student ministry of over five hundred. After I graduated I came back to this town to continue your work. I gave up my pursuit of prestige and money, the career I had studied for and thought I wanted, because I knew the only reason I existed was to spread your good word.

"I turned down many opportunities to join corporate America as I rededicated myself to my hometown and my community. Eventually I left my accounting practice I set up here to being a life serving only you. I started cleaning the church and the prison that I had volunteered at, spreading your grace and love everywhere I went. I thank you again for the blessings of my family and your light. Your guidance allowed me to get up everyday and do your good work. I thank you for the strength you gave me to improve myself everyday. I thank you for the patience and trust you placed in me so I could admit my sins and short comings so I could be forgiven. I owe you everything in my life and could not be more grateful."

Finishing, John looked back up to see Jesus smiling back at

him. Paralyzed John did not have any tears or strength left to express his bliss. So he waited. He sat and waited for his Lord to say something. And after a few tense moments his Lord started to move and speak once again.

"Thank you John. That was very interesting and I see we still have much to talk about."

9. THE SCARY TRUTH

Walking into the bathroom Jill was disgusted that she ever stepped foot in here the night before.

"What was I thinking?" Jill talked to herself, treading softly on the grimy, fluid stained floor. Taking stock of her immediate surroundings Jill made a personal resolution to never find herself in a place like this again.

"It's better than sleeping with Greg," Jill forced a laugh, trying to lighten the mood, as she walked towards the bathrooms sinks. Hoping it would spur her memory back into gear.

At the vanity Jill did not know where to put her hands. Hand prints, ass prints, and god knows what else lived on this seldom cleaned surface. After a minute of searching Jill found a place to rest her hands. Balanced on her hands Jill looked into the mirror and as her own eyes stared back at her, through the grimy reflection, the memories began to flood back.

Walking into the bathroom Jill placed her hands down on the counter.

"God this place is a pit," she thought to herself. "It is cleaner than Greg though… The little asshole."

Looking into the mirror the muffled sounds of the bar accompanied Jill's reflection as she took stock of her situation and tried to think of her way out of this.

"How can I get away? I don't want to wait for a cab, but the bartender won't let me drive. Staying here is not an option. I got to get away from Greg. Somehow."

Behind Jill the door opened. With no inclination of checking who came in Jill continued to ponder her situation as the sounds of the bar faded when the door swung shut.

"How do I get out of this?" Jill thought. The sounds of the bar became louder as the door swung open again. "How do I leave?" Jill thought when the sounds became muffled once again.

Jill had never heard a second or third patron enter the room. Like all of us Jill never thought twice about someone coming to relieve themselves in a bar bathroom."I could always call a friend," was Jill's last thought when it all went hell.

Recoiling from the vanity Jill fell to the floor as she tried to fend off the memories. Little episodes from the night before assaulted her as the hell this bathroom had become came into full view.

Hands were on her shoulders and, before she could turn, her head was being pushed down into the sink in front of her. Startled and unaware of what was going on Jill felt another pair of hands pull her scrubs and panties down. Wanting to scream Jill couldn't. The hand that had been on her shoulder was now covering her mouth. Opening her eyes Jill was face to face with the bottom of the sink, dirt and rust staring her in the face as she felt the horror fill her. "You like this? Hmm? Don't you you little bitch?" Jill heard a distant voice say as she faded into reality.

On the bathroom floor tears filled Jill's eyes as she looked around. Searching the bathroom Jill attempted to find signs that this did not happen to her. She desperately wanted to think that this was a twisted nightmare. Flustered and frantically moving on her hands and knees she found the prints they made the night before as more deplorable memories returned.

No longer in the sink Jill was on all fours. Her mind raced as she wondered how long she had blacked out and when her assailants had moved her. Opening her eyes Jill immediately closed them as she saw another horror approaching her face. "Open your damn mouth. You little bitch," a strange voice told her as she was slapped across the face. The jarring blow forced her mouth open just a little bit. That little opening was all Jill's assailant needed and she soon found herself gagging on the newly protruding invader. "You like the taste you little bitch? Hmm... don't you?" Jill wanted it to be over. Her eyes closed she found herself praying they would finish and it would all be over.

Outside of her memories Jill crawled away from that spot on the floor. Silently hoping that distancing herself from that space would make the nightmare end. In her haste her hand found something that proved last night was not a demented nightmare. Painfully turning her head Jill's heart dropped as her eyes confirmed what she felt: opening her hand she was holding the panties, ripped and torn, that she had worn the night before.

Opening her eyes, Jill felt cheap, sick, and violated. Fluids raced out of her; she did not dare look down to see if it was blood or worse. Eyes full of tears, her vision blurred, Jill watched their shadows leaving. Wanting to move she Jill couldn't and instead saw a shadow throw her panties onto her face, striking her. Jill grabbed the panties and threw them away, never wanting to touch them again. Trying to stand Jill wanted to get help, to get these bastards, but she couldn't move. Outside the door she heard the bar going about its business, normal, undisturbed, no one the wiser to what had just happened. Pulling up her scrubs Jill slowly stood up feeling that this day could not get any worse.

Back in the present Jill's memory failed. She could not remember anything else even though she wanted to. Jill looked around frantically for a towel or something that would spur her memory or possibly give her a clue to who her assailants had been. Unfortunately, Jill found nothing. There was nothing left for her to find. Picking up her panties she stuffed them into her purse praying they would hold evidence that would lead her to her assailant. Leaving the bathroom Jill wanted to talk to the bartender one last time as the memories of the night rolled around in her head.

"Hey barkeep? Who did I leave with last night?" Jill yelled at him, silently wondering what bastard had violated her last night.

"You left with that Greg guy and his friend I think. They both went outside to grab a smoke when you left for the bathroom.

Then a few minutes later Greg was walking you out through the front door. To be honest I was a little surprised considering you had given him the cold shoulder earlier. I mean you looked a mess, but were holding on to him for dear life, so I gave him your keys and let you go."

Horror spread across her face as she tried piece the night back together without any additional flashback or memories. "Could Greg and Andrew gotten into the back, near the bathrooms, without you or anyone else noticing?" Jill asked trying to confirm her fears. Knowing that the bartender kept track of time as well as he cleaned his bathroom.

"Of course. I'm not a damn baby sister or chaperone. The back door is where most people go to smoke and it's right next to the bathroom," the bartender responded as he poured a local drunk his fifth drink of the day.

Wandering out of the bar Jill heard the barkeep yell something about not being responsible for anything that happened. She did not hear what he was saying and did not care. She had more important things on her mind. Had Greg and Andrew raped her? Did something happen when they got home? And why the fuck did she let Greg bring her there?

.

10. QUESTION
OF FAITH

Martin looked away from John as he completed his riveting tale. Like those of Athena and Jesus, John's story was immersive and interesting. He loved listening to and dissecting these stories. It is what he lived for in his search for the truth.

The pain and hardship Mr. Witherspoon had faced drove him closer to his faith. When the going got tough and he began to shut down John never gave up hope or his faith. It was a real sight to see how John's faith had brought him through the rough times. How, despite what his father had done, John had seen a message of love and acceptance behind the gospel, not hate. That was something that interested Martin and if he had a chance he would love to explore that further with John.

Turning towards the judge's bench Martin saw Thor sitting in front of him. The Norse God's appearance was not only imposing, but shocking. Looking at his body, the armor, a helmet and hammer, Martin was so enthralled with investigating Thor's form that he did not hear when Thor began to speak.

"Martin… Hello Martin. Are you there?" Thor's booming voice knocked Martin out of his delusional trance.

"Yes… sir… I'm sorry what were you saying?" Martin quickly recovered.

"I was asking what you thought of John's tale about his faith and how he came to it? Considering you specialty is religious stories and narratives I'm curious what you think?"

Looking at John, Martin did not know how to answer. A second ago he was hoping to discuss John's story, but now, presented with the opportunity, he cringed and wanted to turn away from the invitation. Martin was always skeptical and, while he was excited to hear the story, there were a few holes in it that Martin had to explore before he could give a real response. At the same time however Martin wanted to express his joy with John's story and how honest and sincere it was. He wanted to dive further into John's faith while, in a very blunt way, wanting to be polite.

"Did you hear the question?" Thor asked again.

"I did, I just don't know where to begin…" Martin stuttered a quick answer.

"Why don't you begin with something positive and see where it goes from there," an ominous voice said as if it were coming from the depths of the sea. Looking up Martain saw that Poseidon was now watching the trial.

"That sounds like a good idea," Martin remarked realizing that that was a lot easier said than done.

Gathering his thoughts Martin looked around the court. He knew that every second he didn't say something made things more awkward and would make his stance that much harder to explain. His eyes found intricate flower work indicative of Islamic Mosques interwoven with Osiris and other Egyptian gods at his feet. The bright pedals beauty brought his mind to focus as he began to talk to John.

"On one hand your story is incredible. The way that you acted and persevered through so much while keeping a strong faith is awe inspiring. It reminds me of other narratives I have heard or read in a multitude of traditions. You allowed faith to become a stronghold; a place of rescue and serenity. It is amazing how you let your faith guide you. Impressive how you gave it such an important place in your life."

Looking into John's eyes Martin saw tears well up in them. John was overwhelmed with the fact that Martin recognized how he loved his faith and his Lord. Wanting to let this moment linger the silence was interrupted when Poseidon spoke.

"Is that all?" he asked Martin in a leading tone.

"No…" Martin admitted painfully. "Not exactly. I wonder why John credits so much to his faith. His good character and reaction or lack of reaction could have been disastrous to himself and his sisters. John tells us that you were testing him and his loyalty to his father, but how does that justify the torture and suffering he and, more importantly, his sisters experienced? Why did he never alert the police? Why did he not seek help sooner? Why does he think that the counselor moving in was God's grace? In hindsight all of these things can be attributed to some test of faith, but just as easily can be attributed to a different type of test. What if he had been meant to get help and act on what he knew was right? What if it was not a test at all?

"This is a failure I see in many faith stories where we let the outcome, the conclusion, dictate the moral permissibility to our actions or inactions. Because things worked out well it was the grace of God, but what if his father had continued the abuse? What if his sister had died? What if something more awful had happened? Would that also be your grace? Or would that more likely be John's failure and fault. I wonder how far he has explored those possibilities and others. John talks about starting a faith group in college, that he chose his school because it was devoid of faith, but when he left school he returned home to serve you. He says you guided him away form the sin and corruption of the corporate world to work with the homeless and in the prisons, but doesn't Mathew 5:5 say that: "Blessed are the meek: for they shall inherit the Earth." That you are most with the crippled, the criminal, and the sinner? What if the reason he had opportunities to serve in corporate America was so he could bring faith and good things back to that the private sector in the same way he did at school? We all know they could use a little faith. What proof does he have that that was not actually your plan?"

Taking a breath Martin wanted to continue but the deity, now Moses, cut him off to let John answer.

"He does bring up a good point. Why didn't you contact the police? How did you determine this was some sort of trial? What was my path and what was not?"

Mr. Witherspoon's mind raced. He felt frustrated. He felt attacked. Who was Martin to question him? Why did Martin think he knew more than his Lord and the great book? Looking up at the son John tried to let go of the hate, hurt, and anger festering in his heart. His Lord wanted him to answer Martin's questions so he would.

"Lord. Martin," John started so he could address both of them. "I never called the police because I allowed myself to be guided by your light and scripture. Please do not think that I did not ponder these same things Martin asked. I thought about contacting the police, but it was a different time back then and during these hard times I read scripture and attended bible study religiously. Every time I went to the scripture it spoke to me about my problems and the worries inside of me. It spoke to me about compassion, about loving thy parents, and about assisting those in need. I knew I needed to help my father avoid sin and not simply turn my back on him by reporting him.

"I hid his alcohol. I counseled my sisters. And when he was sober I approached him about his behavior. He was always apologetic and sorry for his behavior. Breaking my family apart would have been turning my back on the Lord and all He taught me. Jesus did not turn his back on the sinners and those who lost their way, he embraced them. That is what Mathew 5:5 is really about. In Exodus 20:12 We are told to: "Honor your father and your mother, so that you may live long in the land the LORD your God is giving you." In the end, that is what I did when I followed the bread crumbs you, my Lord, laid out for me through scripture and study. I do not think it is a coincidence that in my childhood scripture spoke to my plight at the right time. In that way I put my life in your hands and you answered me, you helped me, you loved me, and you saved me. Do I regret not turning my father in? Sometimes I do. However my family is stronger now than I think it would have been if we had broken it up. The Lord helped and guided us," John said his attention focused solely on his Lord. Seeing his Lord smile John gained the strength to continue.

"As to why I avoided going to wall street," John said shifting his focus back to Martin. "I knew that it was not my place. I loved accounting; however, I saw a greater need. I saw a need to show and remind even the most beat down among us, those who felt God had forsaken them the most, His love. I felt a need to share the gospel with them and remind them of His love. In hindsight it is easy to point out that I could have brought the light to a different group of people. But I chose, and was guided down, a life of faith and in many ways poverty. I sacrificed to spread the gospel to those I felt needed to hear it the most."

John finished with a fire and as he sat down Martin felt little comfort in John's answer. John had not addressed the real questions Martin had been hitting at. As Martin saw it pure coincidence allowed everything to work out fine. Blind faith is what Martin saw in John. Any good that happened in his life was God's grace. The hardships were his fault or sin. These questions though were the least of Martin's worries now because at the end of the day both their paths had led them to this place. A place Martin had questioned existing, a place John never had questioned. Before Martin could press further though the deity preempted him with a question to John.

"I see John. Do you have any questions for Martin?"

"If you would allow me to sir I would like to ask him a question." Looking up Jesus nodded opening the door for John to ask. "With everything that you have studied, done, and seen, on Earth and now, how do you or did you decide what was religious myth and what was fact?"

11. THE DEFENDANT'S ACCUSATION

Stunned, Dr. Andrews did not know how to formulate an answer, which surprised him. In his books, study, and even general discussion Martin had always formulated this answer with ease. Normally Martin would tell someone that the truth did not change due to popular belief and there were things that could be established empirically. The topics of physics, biology, chemistry, heck even some sociology and philosophical ideas seemed to fit, but never religion. Every religion was too interpretive and volatile, even if the tenets behind the faith and the lessons were good and true. Religion as an institution, and in many ways faith, was too biased and circumstantial. Standing in the courtroom, at the gates of heaven, those reasons did not seem to resonate however and despite the simplicity of John's question Martin was at a loss.

John asked him: "With everything that you have studied, done, and seen, on Earth and now, how do you or did you decide what was religious myth and what is fact?" For some reason that question was hitting Dr. Andrews hard. How did Martin separate truth in physics, biology, and philosophy? How did he decided what part a religion had right and what part was fiction? He was asking how he accounted for his own bias and in a few words John had turned his question back on him: how did Martin know that God had not answered John's prayers? How did he know that everything that had happened was coincidence? How could he question it considering where they were right now?

Sitting in silence Martin looked up hoping for some clarity and support. But, the walls gave him little comfort as only biblical tales stuck out, making him wonder if there was anything else. Looking to the podium he found Jesus, not Zeus or Athena, starting back at him. Blinking his eyes Martin thought that the light was playing a trick on him, that maybe the deity would change; however, after a minute of blinking nothing changed. Jesus was staring down at him waiting for his answer. Doubt crept into Martin as he struggled to find the words.

"Some things are obviously religious fiction. I'm sure you would agree John that the stories of Osiris ridding the sun across the sky along with Greek God birthing stories are fiction." Looking over at John he saw him nod in agreement. "We have a much better reason for the sun rising and setting everyday than someone dragging it across the sky." A nervous laugh left him as Martin prepared to make his switch, hoping it would get him out of the sticky situation he found himself in. No one else laughed. "In my writings and studies I expounded upon these type of examples and in this same vein every faith has supernatural explanations to things that are simply impossible. For example we all understand that the ingestion of the bread and wine, is only a symbolic gesture and is not really the body and soul of Christ."

John did not nod in approval this time. Martin knew his attempt to side skirt the issue had not worked. It had been a weak argument and while normally eloquent and verbose, in this setting Martin found himself surrounded by doubt as he tried to find a glimmer of his former confidence. Martin was helpless as John opened his mouth to ask him another question.

"You didn't answer my question. I guess what I want to know is what about the Bible and its stories? Why do you think they are all false, whimsical tales? What about my story? Was it just coincidence that everything worked out or was there a higher power at work?" John finished as he nodded towards Jesus.

Following John's nod Jesus was still staring back at Martin. *This has to be a coincidence.* Martin tried to tell himself as he felt the pressure of the question and Jessus's gaze fall on him. Not only had John had asked him to answer the exact question he wanted to avoid, but he had also seen right through his straw man. Ready to reply with an answer worthy of speech Martin knew he could not let this room influence his answer.

"John, the Bible is a very interesting thing in religious studies. As a text it falls in line with several Abrahamic faiths and plays an especially crucial role in Christianity. When I look at the Bible I see a retelling of the same stories and myths that have been around for many millennia." John started raising his eyebrows, but Martin plowed on through his answer. "Sure the characters and location may be different, but the archetypes and messages are the same. When looking at the historical accuracy of a story and if it holds any truth we must look at how the stores were created, passed along, and chosen. The gospels that make up the new testament were hand picked from at least thirteen possible gospels. We have the four main ones that we use in the Bible; however, they themselves and any newly discovered gospels can be quite difficult to rectify each other let alone a cohesive faith.

"Beyond this though the gospels were not being typed, saved, printed, like they are now. The stories were at best hand written by the select few who initially were told and interpreted second hand by someone who heard them. Before literacy became prevalent, stained glass was used to share and create the stories leaving it up to individual priests to retell and reinterpret the story. For generations this is how the Bible was passed down, through the educated few recopying the texts, but the majority of it being retold, shared, and translated through many dialects. A text, fundamental to the creation and succession of power, hand copied and translated multiple times cannot be assumed to be

56

true to its original form. In fact we can only assume that it is vastly changed from what was originally written. A word here or there being changed or miscopied hundreds of years ago and then translated multiple times drastically changes the meaning and reality of any story. Changing a yay too a nay or shall to shall not, puts the stories in different lights and gives them different meanings. Because we cannot verify any of the stories and because many of them are so supernatural I cannot help but be skeptical. Placing all of your cards in this text, all of your truth, would be like placing the answer to the question: "Is the water I am about to drink poisoned?" to a game of telephone that spanned many generations and languages."

John sat silent as he digested what Dr. Andrews had just said. With a sense of momentum Martin utilized the silence to finish his thought.

"Even today, we hold theological debates about the true meaning of a passage. Even if the stories were copied perfectly, how they were interpreted and their overall message has changed with time as societies use the text to justify their own ends. This is not to say that we cannot see something in the text. When we look at its over arching message the bible taps into truths that span many cultures and religions start to emerge. Truth that I feel all religions and faiths tap into at some level. For me, after reading so many texts and embracing so many beliefs it is hard to find greater validity in one over another. In the end they all strike me as myths driving at some central belief or idea."

Martin found John's eyes piercing his soul. Martin knew he had landed a heavy blow to John and was ready for a debate. Unsure who was going to jump first they were both ready to strike when Martin heard Moses voice ring out over the courtroom

"That is enough..." He said. "This is not meant to get hostile. We are having a discussion and sharing our thoughts. Sticks and stones as some would say."

The tension broke as the authority brought civility back into the courtroom. Both of the men visibly relaxed at these words, reminded that they were meant to share and listen. They were not supposed to be attacking each other and becoming defensive was not what this was about.

"Now that you each have had a chance to ask a few questions I would like you to indulge me in something. Down on Earth right now there is an event occurring that you are both linked to. Inside of this little incident there are a lot of issues to sort out and I would like your thoughts and help. As a group I want us to watch and discuss what we think about what is going on. I want us to dig deep together to find the true pillars of our beliefs. If you do this for me afterwards I will have a few questions for both of you before I reveal your eternal fate."

Looking up at the deity Martin and John were stunned. Both fully aware that they did not have much of a choice but to indulge the God before them.

Taking their silence as consent the courtroom changed in the blink of an eye. In an instant God's podium and their tables had disappeared, replaced by a large circular table, with three chairs around it.

"Please come sit, so we can all watch the action going on down there."

Approaching cautiously John and Martin joined the table. Looking into the center of the table, the milky surface showed a scene unfolding on Earth.

12. ACCUSATIONS

Arriving home Jill was surprised her reckless driving hadn't killed someone. Racing up the stairs her thoughts ran faster than she drove. *Had Greg raped her? Did Andrew take part? If they did not rape her who did? Why did she let Greg bring her home? And God forbid what had happened once they got here?*

Even with the discomfort of these disturbing thoughts Jill felt like she was missing something bigger. Jill could not dissuade or dislodge this feeling in the pit of her stomach that something else was seriously wrong.

Walking through her front door Jill's heart sank as she heard the buzzer on the washing machine going off.

"Shit," Jill exclaimed, rushing towards the laundry room, hoping desperately that the buzzer went off by mistake. Hoping that the machine was broken.

Opening the machine she found that the buzzer was not imaginary. Her scrubs that had been full of evidence were now stuck to the sides of the stainless steel canister. Her hopes washed away with her rapist fluids.

"God dammit," Jill exclaimed again. "Why did I wash this shit? I did it this morning because things were a mess and I needed something to do. It was just a reaction, but God dammit I'm stupid. How could I be so blind?"

Berating herself Jill sunk into despair. She had no way of

finding her rapist now. She had no way proving that it was Greg. The bastard would get away with it.

With tears hitting the floor Jill sat there for a minute before she wiped her eyes. "This isn't doing me any good," Jill said to herself. She had never been a weak person and had never given up. What happened may be rough, but she would not let it beat her.

Standing up Jill rededicated herself to piecing the secrets of this nightmare together. She would uncover the truth and punish the person (Greg) responsible. Looking around the washroom Jill did not know where to begin, until she saw a stack of neatly folded sheets next to the dryer.

"Of course," Jill whispered to herself as she ran from the washroom to her bedroom. On the bed laid her undisturbed messy sheets and blankets. She did not wash those this morning. "I've got you now," she thought to herself silently praying that Greg had become greedy and continued his night of vile behavior here.

Rushing to the bathroom Jill was about grab a trash bag to stuff the sheets into a trash bag when she stopped herself.

Her house was a crime scene.

Every glass that was out of place, every blanket, or shampoo bottle. Every towel was possibly evidence. Now standing in the middle of it all Jill wanted to do was get out without disturbing a thing and with that in mind Jill backed left her apartment and locked the doors. She wanted to leave her apartment undisturbed and secure until the police could come and investigate. And while many people's first stop or call would be to the police, Jill was not going there yet. She wanted to give Greg a chance to explain himself, to come clean, and confess before he was disgraced and exposed. Jill was going to go to work first before visiting the local sheriff.

"Jill... what are you doing here?" Sara, Jill's friend and co-worker, whispered to her. Running along side Jill after greeting her at the front door.

"Hello to you too," Jill responded. Power walking towards the hospital's offices.

"Hello?" Her friend responded full of confusion "Jill you are suspended. What the hell do you think you are doing?" Sara said in a hushed whispered, rejecting the clipboards and charts people were trying to hand her.

"I know I'm suspended I just need to know where Greg is," Jill continued while picking up her pace.

"I'm pretty sure he is in a meeting with his father, but."

Jill did not hear another word. Turning down the next hallway she started running towards the dean's office. "Oh how sweet this revenge will be," she whispered as she hurried towards resolution and answers.

Jill was so focussed on revenge she never saw Greg. Five feet from the door as she ran straight into him. Falling to the ground Jill looked up through a sea of papers slowly fluttering to the ground their owner scrambling to wrangle them all. Smiling Jill chuckled to herself. She had found her perp.

"What are you doing here?" Greg asked as he started to gather his papers.

"You know why I'm here. I only wish I had been able to break my news to you in front of your father."

"What news would that be?"Greg asked his voice full of bravado, but with a quiver of doubt.

Now standing Jill took a minute to gather her thoughts. Slightly enjoying watching her rapist's mind circle in fear.

"Oh you know. I was hoping to let your dad know about the

little rapist he raised."

As the accusation left her lips and Greg dropped his papers again.

"SHH…SHH.." Greg panicked as he got closer to her, trying to silence what she had just said.

Trying to escape the gathering crowd Greg gently grabbed Jill's arm and started to lead her towards his office. "Nothing to see here… nothing to see… Emily could you be a doll and pick up those papers and bring them to my dad… tell him I will be right in."

With a smug grin Jill followed Greg's lead to the office. Soon enough everyone would know what he was so there was no reason to fight now. In reality, after last night and how helpless she had felt all day, she was enjoying being in control and was kinda looking forward to watching him grovel. Slamming and locking the door Greg led her to a chair and then took his own before restarting their conversation.

"What the fuck are you talking about Jill…" Greg yelled his temper starting to rise as he tried to take control back.

Sitting smugly Jill actually enjoyed watching him sit there and stew as she gathered her response. Taking her phone out of her pocket and hitting record as she did.

"You know exactly what I am talking about Greg… Last night at my house, at the…"

Waving his hands in the air Greg's assertive anger had turned into panicked fear as he wanted her to stop speaking.Watching him squirm Jill's smile spread with her suspicion confirmed.

So the little bastard raped me again at my house. Jill thought to herself.

Secure in the fact that she knew Greg could not hurt her now. Too many people knew she was in his office. Greg was finally stuck in a situation daddy couldn't buy his way out of.

Still clearly flustered Greg took deep breaths as he prepared his response. "What happened at your place last night… You said was fine… We had an agreement."

His stammered barley coherent answer shocked Jill. All she could remember was her head in being forced into a sink the night before, before she was violated over and over again.

"What agreement was that Greg? The agreement that you and Andrew rape me at the bar and then you take me home to have another go?"

Jill had finally silenced Greg. "What are you talking about at the bar… And what about Andrew…" He finally responded. His quivering voice unable to back his bold face lie about what he had done to Jill the night before.

"You know exactly what at the bar you little shit head. I remember you and Andrew having your fun last night and so does the bartender. Hell even the damn bouncer remembers."

"Jill, you have to let me explain… I don-"

Jill was going to cut him off, but before she could the door opened and two hospital security guards and a deputy were there.

"Are you okay sir?" The sheriff said as he entered. "I heard that there was a commotion.."

"Dave it is fine. We just had a disagreement," Greg tried to reassure them, his face flushed in panic.

"Are you sure sir that she isn't giving you any trouble?"

"Yes it's fine…" Greg again "You can-"

"-Actually don't," Jill cut Greg off. "Dave is it. Could you please get me the sheriff and a detective I would like to report a crime."

"And what crime is that ma'am?"

"Sir, Greg raped me… And my apartment is full of evidence waiting for your team."

13. HARD CHOICES

Doubled over a toilet for the fourth time this week Jill was convinced she had finally located the source of the knot in her stomach. A cause she prayed was wrong. However, Jill was fairly certain she was pregnant.

Getting back to her feet Jill looked into the mirror and reflected on the last couple of weeks trying to understand how she got to this point: standing alone in her bathroom holding a little piece of plastic that she needed to pee on.

After her confrontation with Greg life sped up. She was brought to the sheriffs station where she was interviewed, after which she took a brief trip to the hospital for an exam and then returned to the station house. Detectives stopped by to ask her a few questions, retrieve her keys, and get the name of the bar for a third time. They were nice, courteous, and kept her comfortable. Around six Jill was brought to a hotel, on the city's dollar, because her apartment had become an active crime scene.

Over the next few weeks her story became prime time news, especially after the arrests, something that happened much quicker than she had ever expected. It only took a week before Greg and Andrew were arrested and charged. Her story along with statements from the bartender, bouncer, and a few of the patrons from that night all implicated Greg and Andrew. No one saw them take a smoke and everyone saw them disappear and reappear with her. These eye witness accounts were just the tip of the iceberg. Jill's apartment turned out to be a treasure trove of evidence as they found DNA everywhere, including a mix of Greg's semen and blood on Jill's bed sheets. They found Greg's hair in the drain traps and his fingerprints all over the house, on cups and shampoo bottles alike. After the week the cops had more than enough for the warrant and arrested both Greg and Andrew, hoping one would flip on the other.

Despite Greg's attorney's best intentions to get the cases thrown out, they could not. Greg made bail and was living under house arrest with an ankle monitor. Andrew was waiting for his day in court in county lock up.

What surprised Jill most was that the arrests never loosened the knot in her stomach. At first she thought it had been related to a fear. Fear that the guys would get away with it, but they were behind bars and had a criminal and civil case pending against them. Caught up in the excitement Jill hardly realized she had missed a period, but when she missed two, the full picture became too clear.

Sitting on the edge of her bed Jill was waiting for the results as she fought the questions and emotions that swelled inside of her: *Is it Greg's baby? Am I pregnant? Is it my husband's? Will Greg want custody? What if the baby is not either of theirs? What if Greg hadn't raped her?*

These questions were painful as they shot through her head, but sitting here, waiting, Jill could not help but be brought back to the day of her rape kit. At the hospital they had offered her a plan b pill she politely refused. She never thought that she would be pregnant from this. She was willfully ignorant of that facts. She was still trying to deny what had happened and she never let herself imagine that she could be pregnant. That sort of thing wouldn't happen to her. She even went as far as blaming stress for her missed period, but now, now she sat on a bed waiting for a piece of plastic to possibly change the fate of her life she knew that all of those things before were just wishful thinking.

Since their marriage Jill and Jeff had been trying to start a family with little success. Now that she had missed two periods she hoped beyond hope that it was his, however, she knew the child was not. Maybe their struggles is why she refused the pill. She could not risk losing their baby; however, what if it was her rapist's baby? How could she possibly carry it to term? How could she love a child created out of such tragedy and pain? Jill understood what this all meant, but she also understood this town.

There was no clinic and no one who would support her if she chose to terminate the pregnancy. After refusing that pill Jill understood what she was choosing. The closest clinic was over a hundred miles away and considering that the media was standing outsider her door she would never be able to get away with it without someone noticing.

Jill did not want the talk of the town to be about her abortion. In this area a jury of her peers would condemn her abortion over anything Greg and Andrew did to her. These cynical fears were only reinforced by her growing legal team as they reminded her many times that: "if she was pregnant *a miscarriage*" would be acceptable and believable. An abortion would ruin her all the cases. Unfortunately it would poison the jury she was about to face." Somehow though these things were the least important considerations for her right now. She barely cared about the case. All she wanted to know was what the little stick was going to say.

The idea that the child may not be her husbands and the fear of wondering if he would help her raise it. Wondering how she could possibly raise her rapist's baby while also questioning why she was even considering an abortion were all more pressing than a court case. If she saw this pregnancy through, she would be responsible for another life, another human being on this Earth. That is what was most important.

The seconds ticked into an eternity as Jill waited for the results. Staring at the clock she watched the hand turn

8:42….43…..44….. Until finally 8:45 rolled around and her fate was ready to be revealed. 8:46..8:49… Jill sat paralyzed on her bed not ready to find out the results.

At 8:53 Jill rose from the bed and walked towards the bathroom. At this point she had to know if she was carrying a child. She had to know if her rapist had left something more inside her. Sitting on the counter was a little plastic wand ready to tell her her fate. Walking towards the sink Jill looked into the mirror once before she glanced down ready to take whatever consequences awaited her. A glance told her everything she needed to know. Jill broke into tears as she slumped back against the bathroom door crying as she slid towards the floor.

14. CONCEPTION

The image on the table faded with the girl crying in her car outside an abortion clinic; frozen and confused about what to do next. At the table John and Martin relaxed into their chairs. Looking towards the table's third party John saw his Lord waiting to start a dialogue, while Martin saw Hades preparing to lead the conversation.

"What do you two think the right thing to do is and Why? Who is responsible for this situation Jill finds herself in?" The Entity asked without any pretense or hesitation.

Hearing the question John looked to Martin and back to his Lord. He was waiting for Martin to answer, but wondered if Martin was waiting for the same thing. After a few moments John decided he need to say something. So did Martin.

"She should not get it," they both said in unison.

Surprised, they both recoiled in their chairs and looked back at one another. The Entity looked between the two with whimsical surprise. "Well, now I'm interested," the Deity exclaimed. "John why don't you start us off."

Looking up to his Lord, John took the invitation to begin his explanation.

"In my own studies of your word; your teachings I feel that the signs she saw were spot on. You tell us not to kill. You tell us that the person who has not sinned can cast the first stone. Personally

I think in this situation we can apply those ideas. Jill will only answer to you and you alone, and in the end deciding to end her pregnancy, to take that child's life, is to play God. That soul, that budding being inside of her, needs to be protected. The baby needs to be given life and your good word. For her to have an abortion, well I hope she doesn't because, she simply cannot question your gift like that. She admitted to wanting a child and now she has one. Despite what happened to her it is a blessing that she can now bring another life into this world, a life she can shape and share your word with."

Ending his statement Martin was ready to jump in when Hades raised a question towards John before Martin could speak.

"What if the child has no soul yet? What if it would feel no pain and simply is a collection of cells?"

John gasped at the question. This thought, though it may have nagged him once or twice, was something he had always dismissed. He had never thought it a possibility, but now, The Lord, his savior, was asking him exactly that.

"It is still not her place my Lord. The child inside of her is a creation of yours. A vessel that I am assuming will one day harbor a soul?" John looked up and saw his Lord simply nod in agreement."And to destroy that being would be to remove that soul's chance at that life. Beyond that how is she supposed to know when it goes from being a collection of cells to a person, no matter how she says it, she would still be playing God. She has no way know that the life growing inside of her does not already posses a soul. Ignorant of the facts, killing the vessel or the soul is one in the same. It is not her place to do your role. She should be a shepherd for your good word and blessing. She should care for that child as one of your gifts. The blessing that the child is."

"So John you feel that intention is what matters here. In a sense the outcome of anything is out of your hands and, instead, in mine. All we can control or act upon is what we know; what we intend. What you are telling me is that the consequences of those actions are entirely out of one's control?" The Entity tried to clarify John's thoughts.

"Yes my Lord," John replied. "We can never know what will happen or what you have planned. We must trust you and your plan for us. All we can control is our intentions and thoughts. Our actions and the results of those actions are in your hands, so it is our intentions that matter. The rest is out of our control and is up to you."

Looking up John thought he saw a smile forming on his Lord's face. Looking away John smiled himself. This was harder than he expected it to be, but he was so happy that he was being given the chance to show his devotion. A chance to show his strength and his faith.

"John, your answers are insightful and I thank you for them. Now Martin, would you care to share your answer or is it the same as John's?"

Martin's attention had gotten away from him. John's views on freewill and determinism were fascinating and had drawn him in. They had invigorated him so much that he had forgotten where he was and what they were talking about. All he wanted to do was discuss John's ideas more. However, the Virgin Mary asking him a question, brought Martin back to the reality at hand.

"I do not agree with John's reasoning, but do agree with his choice," Martin started. "Jill is so uncertain of her choice so she should not do something so life altering. All of her questions, thoughts, and fears are valid, but to let a blanket doctrine decide for her is impractical and misguided. This is a unique situation that she must deal with for the rest of her life. The consequences of her choice will impact her for the rest of her life. The real reason that I think she should not go through with it has nothing to do with the idea of fate or souls, but everything to do with doubt. She is uncertain, she is on the fence, and this is not something she can walk back from. This is not a car that she can return. This decision is too important to make filled with this much doubt."

"Jill's decision is out of my control then? The consequences? What if the child had a soul? Does that change anything? If not her faith and her values, where should she get the guidance, knowledge, and support she needs to make her decision?" The Entity asked Martin.

"The decision she makes at this point must be out of concern for her own wellbeing and the possible wellbeing of the life inside of her. With that said this is her decision. I do not believe that this is some sort of test or that you have control of the consequence. There is no evidence to support either of those ideas. This type of situation is not unique to Christianity and pops up throughout time in different liturgies. Every time we discuss abortion or ending a pregnancy it is never black and white, but always gray. This concept is gray just like many of the commandments. The idea that thou shall not kill gets thrown out the window when we bring up justifiable war. Love and respect thy mother and father takes on many forms if the mother or father is abusive," Martin commented not meaning to hit a nerve with John. "Jill is battling with a decision that will alter her and the possible life inside her for the rest her and its possible life. A decision of this magnitude should be made with careful thought and consideration, not blindly in the back of a sedan, full of confusion and doubt," Martin continued, starting to get worked up, as the Entity, now appearing as Mother Mary, continued to press him.

"I see Martin, but what of her responsibility to the life inside of her? Does that life not count or have a voice? You keep talking about her, her, her, but then mention and quickly dismiss the life inside her. Beyond that and more importantly where should she gather guidance from?"

Inside Martin laughed a little as the Deity nailed him down again. The Deity was pressing him for the details that he fought hard to avoid. Martin did not know where the right place for the woman to find guidance was. He knew where he would search, but he recognized that he was not everyone.

"From experience, knowledge, logic, trust, and gut," Martin started. "She should ask for help from those she trusts and find solace in sources that can help guide her. This will help bring her to the choice that is the right for her. Ignorance is a two- headed beast. Ignorance about her making a rash decision is a risk, like John pointed out, but all encompassing the blind faith is just as dangerous. Any faith, ideal, or supposed truth that cannot hold up to scrutiny and questions, that shies away from them, is not very strong. It would do her and the child inside her a disservice for her not to think about this situation from many different angles; for her to battle and think hard about this issue. Knowledge will find her a reason and, truth. As for her responsibility towards the child, I can honestly admit my ignorance and say I do not know."

Martin sat back down calmer than when he stood. He thought he explained himself as he looked past Mother Mary towards the luminescent wall and the image of Mount Olympus. Relaxing Martin looked back to see John, looking down, shaking his head a little bit.

"We are from two different places," Martin thought to himself.

Seeing John avoiding eye contact though was aggravating. Not because Martin was filled with pity or anger, but because he felt insecure and vulnerable. Despite all of his claims to knowledge Martin felt like a Platonic scholar who was questioning everything. He felt like he had nothing to fall back on. Martin slightly envied John's dedication, trust, and strength in his held belief. From where Martin sat, John had answers that he trusted. Martin felt like his answers fell short, especially if the fetus was actually alive.... If it was then... Well then what was Martin arguing for?

15. SIMPLE TESTS

Jill was exhausted as she walked into the courtroom for the hundredth time. It had been a long few months as Jill was finally starting to show. Today she sat behind the DA instead of next to her attorney. With two cases going on, the criminal and civil, a day did not go by where Jill was not in a courtroom or with some sort of lawyer.

Maybe today, Jill thinks to herself. *Maybe today will be the day when the bastard must defend himself on the stand.*

The trial had moved very rapidly. She was not sure if it was the high profile nature of the case, or money greasing the wheels of justice, but the trial itself seemed to be fast tracked, well it had been.

After the initial arrest and investigation charges where brought quickly, mostly from Greg's father pressuring the DA to charge his son or let him go. Thinking he could get it thrown out Greg's father pushed for a quick resolution, using media and money to share what he called his son's unlawful plight. Of course after the case was not thrown out, after it was not dismissed, it left his son vulnerable. The trial began, the prosecution presented their case, and now the defense was dragging its feet. Trying to buy time to finalize their defense for a case they hoped would have been dismissed.

Jill was actually looking forward to Greg's defense. He never denied that they had sex, in her bedroom, and instead he vehemently denied that he had ever raped her. In the press he claimed they had consensual sex that night. That was why his fluids and fingerprints were all over everything. For his part Greg's lawyer kept pushing the theory that there was a second man who had raped Jill in the bar bathroom. Unfortunately the evidence didn't support that. Greg and Andrew didn't have an alibi and their fingerprints and hair were found on the door and in the bathroom itself.

God I'm ready for this to continue. Jill thought to herself as the courtroom filled. That actually happening was doubtful today. The case was being held up for the paternity test.

The test had been invasive and had monumental consequences. Jill had resisted at first saying she was not ready to be poked and prodded more, when in reality she was not ready to put her child in danger. However, she did eventually give in after much pushing from her own team and assurances from the doctors that everything would be fine.

The test could be the final nail that they needed to put Greg or Andrew away. If it was not them they would have the DNA of her assailant. Sitting on a court bench, clutching her growing belly, Jill thought about what the test would mean.

Was Greg the father? What about custody? Child support? Possible visitation? If it was Greg, would she get her job back? What would her husband say? Did it matter who the father was? What if it was Andrew? Or what if it wasn't either of them?

"All rise," the words came from the bailiff bringing Jill back from her thoughts to the full courtroom.

The Judge entered, took his place, and asked everyone else to do the same before directing the same question to the defense for the fourth day in a row: "Defense are you ready to proceed?"

Greg's lawyer began to rise and Jill could hear his words before he uttered them "Your honor, you know about the paternity test being performed. The results are not available and play a pivotal role in this case and we request a stay until such evidence has arrived and we all have had ample time to look over it."

The court turned back to the Judge. This was an important decision, another day would be unprecedented, but Jill knew that his answer would be the same as yesterdays.

"While I hesitate to give more time, I do recognize the importance of the test; however, it remains true that it does not and should not decide this case, nor does it dictate the defense," the Judge started.

The Judge was clearly perturbed with the defense team, he was laying it on a little harder into them today; however, Jill didn't think much of this and knew that it probably wouldn't matter. She just waited for the Judge to finish his ruling.

"However, due to the importance of this case and due to the fact that part of this delay is the responsibility of the defendant I ask you Miss Alarosa, do you have any objection to this? Or better yet do you have any knowledge of where the test is?"

Looking back to the young DA prosecuting her case, Jill waited, like everyone else, for Ms. Alarosa answer.

"Your honor we should have the results some time today; however, I would like to proceed. The defense first pushed this court for a speedy trial and has now dragged its feet. Everyday they try their case in the court of public opinion and that is not fair to our victim. Regardless of the results the defense has to continue their defense or rest and let the jury decide."

Jill could read the Judge's mind as he weighed the pros and cons. The paternity test was important, but not critical. If Greg or Andrew wasn't the father the prosecution would have lost some evidence; however, Greg and Andrew would still have plenty to answer for.

"I think it is best we wait. It is Thursday and with a long weekend coming up I give both councils this message: Tuesday we resume the trial with or without a test," the Judge declared. Striking his gavel the Judge began to rise as Greg's attorney began to object.

"Your honor, that test is a turning point in this case. If my clients are not the father then-"

"-Then they still have to explain semen in her bed and any other evidence against them. Just because it is possible that Jill was raped by a third man does not mean that your clients are innocent. You have had an extra week to prepare Mr. Billingsly and you should take the time as a gift."

16. ONE SIDED

The weekend flew by and Jill found herself back in the same seat as the courtroom filled in around her. The test results came in Friday afternoon and Jill had spent a lot of the weekend crying into a pillow. The results frustrated her, but the more she cried the more she realized that there was not a result that would not have frustrated her. Before long the Judge entered, the trial resumed and Greg was on the stand ready to defend himself.

"So Mr. Crasnick, I do not think we need to start with any pleasantries. We all know your father, we all know what you have been accused of, and how hard this has been on you and your family. So why don't you start by telling us, in your own words why you were outside the bathroom in the back of the bar?"

Gathering himself the courtroom went quiet as Greg began to speak. "I was outside, taking a smoke, with Andrew. I know it is a dirty habit, but it is something I have struggled to stop." The pity in his voice was already creating the persona he was going to present today. He had been coached and was more ready for this than Jill had been.

"I see, so do you think it would have been possible you touched the door, of the bathroom Jill was in, on your way outside?"

"Of course," Greg answered his lawyer's question to try and talk away the fingerprint found at the scene. "I distinctly remember tripping on my way out and reaching for the door to get my balance. As for the hair found in the bathroom, I have no idea how that got in there, but it wasn't anything but a hair off my head. It could have fallen off Mrs. Harris that night, we had been close on the bar, or possibly the next morning when she returned."

You bastard.... Jill thought to herself. He knew that that scenario was unlikely. His hair was in that bathroom because he raped her in that bathroom with his friend. Looking at the jury Jill was having a hard time judging if they were buying it.

"And you told the police all of this?"

"Of course I did, but I am not a detective that is not my job. All I know is that I tripped and went out back for a smoke."

"So after you stepped outside to smoke what happened?"

"I needed to use the bathroom before we left the bar. So Andrew and I went back in and that is when Jill, I mean Mrs. Harris, stumbled out of woman's bathroom in tears. I had no idea what had happened to her, but she looked bad. She looked like she needed a friend. Instead of going to the bathroom I took hold of her, so she wouldn't fall down, and asked her what happened. She didn't say anything. I asked her if she wanted to go to the hospital, I even offered to bring her; however, she refused and told me that she did not want to go. She told me that she just wanted to be held and kept safe."

Jill's stomach turned in knots as she watched her rapist begin to spin his little tale. The DA and counselors had told her this would happen and tried to prepare her, but listening to it, Jill realized there was no way to prepare to hear someone lie about raping you. Jill, of course, had no memory of this and it matched what the bartender had told her. Looking away from Greg to, the back of, the DA Jill got a little solace in the fact that Greg would have to answer her questions too.

"So after she refused your offer what happened?"

"I helped her move away from the bathroom and waved to the

bartender. Jill collected her keys only after I assured the bartender I would be bringing her home. We went out to her car, I helped her in, and then we drove to her place. Andrew took my car and left for the night."

"So, Mr. Crasnick, to clarify, neither you nor Mr. Laftis sexually touched Mrs. Harris at the bar? Nothing sexual happened between any of you at the bar?"

"Yes sir, that is correct," Greg responded.

"If that is the case sir then can you explain why your DNA was found all over Mrs. Harris's bed? Can you please explain how you came to be the father of her unborn children?"

A gasp filled the air as the court finally heard the missing piece of evidence for the first time. Greg was the father. Small talk erupted in the courtroom as Jill ignored the glances, points, whispers, and stares coming her way. Instead she did what her lawyer told her to do, stare at Greg and wait for his response.

The sound of a gavel silenced the courtroom's innocuous hum as Greg prepared his rehearsed answer.

"Once we arrived back at her place, I helped her into her apartment, into her bedroom, before using her guest bathroom to relieve myself. After I was done I was about to leave, but wanted to make sure Mrs. Harris was okay so I entered her bedroom through the open door. Jill, sorry, Mrs. Harris was on her bed crying, sobbing. As a friend, I walked over to her and put my arm around her and asked her what was wrong. We have been friends for many years now and I wanted to help a friend in need."

Friends!!! Friend???? Are you fucking kidding me?!?! Jill thought to herself as she listened to Greg explain his actions.

"Jill..Mrs Harris, I'm sorry I am new to this," Greg reminded the court with his boyish ignorance and charm. His face contorting in deep thought as he stopped talking.

"What is it?" Greg's lawyer asked.

"It is just, when I heard that the child was mine, well it makes the formal titles harder. Especially when I remember that night. You see Jill was babbling inaudible words. She was under a lot of stress. Her husband had just been deployed, she had been suspended from work, and had seen one of the worst accidents this town has ever seen earlier that morning. It seemed like she needed someone to hold her, so I did, as a friend. I did that for a while and then one thing led to another. She looked up at me and kissed me. In her fragile state I did not want to cause her any more pain so I kissed her back. I swear to you that what we did next was mutual and has led to a great gift. I was weak, but she was and is a close friend. And I was only following her lead," Greg said motioning towards Jill . "After we had finished Jill fell asleep in my arms, peaceful, and calm. After she was asleep I showered, dressed, and left."

Greg rested is hands on his lap, trying to look the hero and it disgusted Jill. He had twisted everything and Jill hoped that the jury would see past his practiced charm and playful ignorance. In her mind Greg had just made her out to be an unstable, married drunk who had taken advantage of her friend with her slutty tendencies, worst of all his testimony was not over.

"Do you regret what happened that night?" Greg's lawyer asked.

"Yes and no. Part of me regrets doing it because it was a sin; however, part of me is very happy about this moment. We had a beautiful moment, I know that Jill and her husband were having problems, and while I never want to break them up I must admit that I want to be a true father to my children. Jill will have her wish, she gets to be a mother. It is a gift from God. I know how much she wanted a child and now she will have two."

Another gasp came as Greg told the court the other juicy piece of information: Jill was having twins.

"So it is your testimony that your sexual encounter with the defendant was consensual?"

"Yes sir."

"And you have no idea who violated her in the bathroom and you also had no knowledge of that event ever taking place that night?"

"Yes sir… If I knew who did it I would be out there right now hunting those guys down. No one who hurt the mother of my children would ever get away with that."

On a roll, the lawyer continued.

"And you mentioned Jill and her husband having issues with their marriage."

"Objection your honor. Hearsay."

Jill was grateful, it was the first time the DA had objected, and even though she had told Jill that she probably wouldn't object much, it made her feel a little better knowing that Greg and his team had overstepped.

"Your honor it goes to Greg's interpretation of the situation and his perception. As for it being hearsay we can confirm that Jill has not told her husband about this whole situation and have witnesses from his unit who can discuss this strained relationship."

Jill gasped at this as the DA threw up her hands and objected again. The courtroom becoming a flurry of commotion after Greg's attorney's last statement.

Striking his gavel the court calmed as the Judge invited both counsels up.

"Your honor, that was an underhanded tactic and…"

"- You do not need to go on Miss Alarosa. I agree; however, I think that the question does have some bearing on the case so I will allow it. However, Mr. Billingsly you know better and try a trick like that again and I will have you brought up on disciplinary charges."

Jill watched the Judge talk and when Ms. Alarosa turned she could tell from her gait that she had lost the argument. Greg was going to get to answer.

"Again how did you interpret the relationship between Mrs. Harris and her husband? And how did that affect your state of mind and the situation?"

"I had know for a while that Jill had a strained relationship with her husband. His being away, not being able to help her with the pressures of her job, and their inability to conceive.would stress anyone. On the night in question it was obvious that Jill was longing for the type of comfort she would have received from her husband, but yet again he was not there. I have always had feelings for Jill, everyone knows that, and maybe at times I was too forward, but I did not want her hurting herself, I did not want her alone, and I wanted what was best for her."

Jill scowled, the little liar knew nothing about her life. He was assuming and even had implied that she was one to harm herself or commit suicide. Calming herself Jill thought of the one positive: her lawyer would have a turn.

"One more question, is there any reason why you have not assisted Jill in getting her job back? You are a major part of the hospital and it would seem odd that you would leave the mother of your children suspended and without recourses."

Jill was shocked by the question, what was he getting at? Why would his lawyer bring this up?

"The reason that she has been without recourses is she has never reached out to me or my family. It has been lawsuit this and lawyer that. In fact the morning after we spent our night together she raced to my office to accuse me of this horrible crime. She never wanted to talk or to hear my side of the story. Ever since I left her house that night I have been dealing with this horrible ordeal. When Mrs. Crasnick found me that morning I was going to discuss her suspension and the investigation with my father. Unfortunately the legal trouble here has interfered with our investigation. As much as I care for Jill, and would even venture to say love her, I take my hospital and my job very seriously. We are responsible for the health and the safety of the people in this town. To let Jill back without the proper investigation would put all of us at risk. It would be disservice to the community that we strive to protect. No amount of legal pressure will get her her job. Like everyone else Mrs. Crasnick must go through proper channels and procedures. No one will pressure us to putting more lives in risk. However, please do not think that Mrs. Crasnick has been without resources or help, we reached out this weekend after we found out that the children were mine. We did what we could to end this, through the proper channels of course. Beyond that if Jill ever needed anything all she ever had to do was ask."

Jill almost vomited as Greg smiled at her. He was a slimeball. Greg had reached out, he reached out to tell her he was filing for joint custody. Something her lawyers were ready for and already planning to fight.

"Is there anything else you would like to say to the court?"

"To the court not really, but to Jill yes. And considering how hard it has been to talk to her lately and how twisted my actions have become I do have something I would like everyone here to hear me say."

"Your honor," the DA started to object as she rose from her seat. "This is not appropriate for a rapist to address his victim in the courtroom."

"Sir, he is an alleged rapist and please give my client a chance. If he oversteps you can cut him off," Greg's lawyer offered a compromise.

In the court, eyes turned from the Judge to Greg, and back to Jill who now stared at Greg as if she were trying to pierce his soul and read his mind.

What could this bastard have to say? Jill thought to herself as the court's eyes darted back and forth between her and Greg.

The Judge weighed his options before finally nodding yes to Greg, allowing him to continue.

"First, I would like to say that I am sorry for everything that has happened to Jill. Despite her accusations, I do not love her any less and I want to, and plan on, being a part of my children's life. And with her blessing I would like to support them both in any and every way that I can."

Her stomach wrenching, wishing her lawyer would stop this, Jill could hardly listen to any more as Greg continued to speak.

"I still love Jill, and... And I want to be a part of her life. I forgive her for all of this and hope she can forgive me. I hope that she can see my offer as the olive branch that it is and not part of some twisted plot. I do not know if she is afraid of her husband, but I offer her any protection she needs and any help she needs in getting out of the relationship. I know she may never love me how I love her, but I hope that eventually she may give me a chance to show her that I can be the perfect father, friend, and possibly more. If God permits."

Greg sat patiently as the court ingested what he said. Jill felt awful. In a matter of minutes Greg had made her feel like a hussy, while making himself out to be a fallen knight. He made his intentions clear about the children and had even cast a shadow about her marriage.

Greg was the gracious friend, the misguided lover who acted impulsively once. He had laid everything that had happened as a part of God's master plan. Jill hated him for all of it and everything he had just said. Greg was a bastard, a jerk, a rapist, and above all believable. That made it worse. He even had her questioning herself and her decisions. She had been unable to get pregnant with her husband and was it possible all of this was a misunderstanding? Was she resisting God's plan by destroying the name of her children's father.

17. RESPONSIBILITY

Looking up from the center of the table John saw his Lord, sitting in front of him, ready to continue the discussion. Martin saw Mars, the God of war, waiting.

"Before we finish watching the case unfold I think we should explore something further, mainly: Who do you think is responsible for what happened to Jill? Martin why don't you start us off this time?"

Taking a deep breath Martin nodded to Mars and began.

"I do not think that she can be held accountable for being raped, any arguments used to defend this stance are biased and sexist. We would never blame a baby for being kidnapped and trying to place the blame on the victim is simply preposterous. You cannot control the heinous nature of someone inserting their will over you to harm or do something criminal. With that said, and I think you are touching at this, while she is not responsible for the initial attack, she is responsible for her reactions to everything that has happened since. When it comes to that, I think she can be held responsible for how she reacts and responds to this situation."

"She never knew that going to the bar would lead to such a horrific night that would change her forever. All that she wanted was a chance to unwind, relax, and escape from the world. I can guarantee you she will never drink that much ever again, if at all. Again we cannot hold her responsible for getting raped in a bathroom and in her bedroom as well."

Martin paused realizing that he was repeating himself. Taking a breath Martin tried to control his nerves, keenly aware that this conversation, that his trial was closer to the end than the beginning.

"With that said, the trial, confronting Greg and Andrew, resisting their efforts to reach out, choosing to have the baby, press charges, not telling her husband all of those things were her choice. That is not to say that she made the right or wrong decisions, but that they were her choices to make. To go at this alone without her family, her husband, that is her choice. I am not condemning her, but merely pointing out that they were her choices. How she feels, thinks, and responds to this situation, how she lets these things change and shape her are partly in her control. The choice to get counseling or help to sort those sorts of things out certainly is in her control and is something she can be held responsible for."

Finishing Martin looked up to see Arch Angel Michael ready to push him.

"Wouldn't you hold a drunk driver accountable for his actions? It was her choice to go to the bar that night. She could have gone home; read a book, drank there, invited friends over. Isn't everything that happened a consequence of her choice to go to the bar? Her choice to drink to excess?"

Martin was about to answer, when John spoke up.

"Being raped was not her choice. I have a lot of experience with drunks and many times they have no concept or care about the consequences of their actions or their choices. Jill; however, tried to be responsible by at least turning in her keys. Could she have made a different choice, of course she could have, but what happened in that bathroom was rape."

"And the bedroom?" The Entity questioned John.

"Well, there is more gray there, but if she didn't want it, if she didn't lead him on, and assuming he was not too drunk himself to make the decision, then there could have been a crime there as well. To me though, in no way was she acting like an irresponsible drunk. On the contrary, I like to think that she had learned from her prior experience at that bar and did all she could to avoid that happening again."

A little shocked Martin was staring at John. He was surprised. And while he felt that maybe he was leaving too much room in the case of what happened in the bedroom, John was still conceding that it could have been rape. Considering his beliefs Martin was sure he would place the blame on Jill, it was her choice to go to that bar even after what had happened the time before, she chose to go to a place she knew was not the best. To his surprise though John did not say or feel this. Maybe it was because of his own upbringing and experience, maybe he did not realize that what he said about Jill was at odds with some of his previously stated beliefs, regardless Martin smiled as he remembered something all his studies had told him: He should not judge a book by his cover. He should never assume.

"So do you agree with John then?" The Entity, who now appeared to Martin as Moses once again, pushed.

"What happened that night is not her fault. She was trying to be safe and responsible. Was going to the bar a poor choice? Maybe, but we cannot live with expectation that we are going to be harmed for going out. Women cannot expect to be raped multiple times in a night simply because they drank. She had given up her keys, she paid the bouncer off for protection, she did everything she knew to be safe and just wanted to let off steam instead of going home to am empty house. She could have gone home, but what good would that have done her? She had a horrible day, her husband was gone, and she probably did not want to sit in an empty house alone."

"You said that already Martin. What about what happened back at her home?"

"I do not agree with John on everything. Greg, despite his testimony so far, knew that Jill was drunk and not in her right mind. He never should have taken advantage of her like that. Is it possible, even probable, that he attacked her in the bathroom? Yes, but even if he didn't, what he says happened in the bedroom is not any better. Jill was not in a state to give consent. Greg allowed his base desires to overcome his common sense and any moral code. Despite his testimony I still think Greg is holding something back. There is more to his story than meets the eye. It is too perfect. The one thing Jill's character has shown is that she is truthful, Greg simply isn't. He tries to present this face that he made some mistakes, but did nothing criminal. He seems to think he can be observant enough to see that his *"friend"* needed help and a shoulder to cry on. That she needed a way out of her marriage, but couldn't see that she was drunk? His story walks the line of bad judgment and criminal and I think that is just to convenient."

"I see, so the drunk driver is not responsible then?" The Entity pushed Martin.

"It is apples and oranges. She did all she could to protect those around her and herself. She did not drive, she was not hostile, she was just trying to relax. Because people took advantage of her vulnerable state does not mean she did anything wrong. The drunk driver, the abusive alcoholic, know the consequences of their drinking and place themselves in those situations anyways. Even if the person is not an alcoholic, but chooses to drive after drinking, then they are making a choice that puts others in danger. Being willfully ignorant of the facts is very different from not knowing the future."

Looking up Martin waited for Moses. He felt jumbled and out of sorts. He felt like he had just run a marathon and tried to catch his breath and his thoughts. He knew he had repeated himself multiple times, but wondered if he had made any sense. Waiting for another question Martin was surprised when the Entity nodded his head and looked towards John.

"Would you like to expand on what you said earlier John?"

Looking away from Martin, John took the question form his Lord and nodded as he began to speak.

"Lord, while I agree that she could not control being raped. What Martin said about drunks has well, changed my mind in a way. You see she knew the sin, frivolity, and underclass seediness that bar bred. She placed herself there and even if she did not know what was going to happen she did place herself in a bad situation. She never thought she would get raped, but she knew what that place bred. I am not saying she asked for it, but she turned to sin in her time of need instead of you. I am not condemning her for what she did, I'm not saying she deserved it, but again she knew what that place was. I feel that she could have possibly made a different choice."

"I am not sure what you are saying?" The Entity asked John. "Are you blaming her? Is she responsible or is she not?"

"Well, my Lord, first I am not one to judge-'" John started to say when his Lord interrupted him.

"-I understand that, but I do want to understand where you are coming from," his Lord forcefully asked John to continue to clear his statement. "Even if it comes across as harsh or judging I want to see your heart, and what you truly think."

Martin felt like a fly on the wall as John and the Entity seemed to have completely forgotten about him. Watching John gather himself Martin was very interested in seeing John's answer and how the Entity would take it.

"She sinned when she got home," John started. "I do not know if she lead Greg on, I do not know if something else happened, another side to the story may exist, but she does not remember and I have not seen anything that makes me think her lack of a tale is more plausible than Greg's. They both sinned, but blaming it on the alcohol, on being drunk, is no excuse. She was the one who made the choice to drink and she must take responsibility for what happened. She placed herself in the situation. Do I think she was raped in the bathroom, I do, but Greg's story simply put is not a story of rape, possibly regret, but not rape. And again it was her choice to go to that bar. She knew what that place was like and, I guess, that makes her somewhat responsible for what happened to her that night."

Martin was wondering if the Entity was going to push John on his wavering words; however, he did not. Instead the Entity was smiling at John.

"I think we should rejoin the trial."

18. HE SAID, HE SAID

The DA buttoned and straightened her jacket as she approached the witness. Jill looked up from the gallery with little hope. *I hope she can show this man's true colors.* She thought to herself as the DA began to speak.

"So you say that you will support her? Why haven't you done so yet? What exactly are your intentions once the children are born?"

Greg sat in silence waiting for his lawyer to object, when he didn't, Greg answered.

"I will, and I would have, if she asked. Jill has not asked for any assistance and considering the lawsuits I assumed she wanted to have nothing to do with me. I thought that she must be doing fine on her own."

"Really? You think an unemployed, alone, pregnant woman, being dragged in and out of court is doing well? A woman who is carrying her rapist's babies. You think she is doing fine?"

"Objection your honor," Jill heard Greg's lawyers yell out.

"Sustained," the Judge said agreeing that the DA was overstepped her bounds with her accusation.

"So you really think that she is doing well?" The DA asked again without some of the modifiers.

"I think that she is making her own choice and has not reached out to me in any way. From what I can see she looks healthy."

Looking a little dejected the DA wanted to object to something, but couldn't. She gathered herself and pressed on.

"Once the kids are born what do you envision your role in their lives being? What are you after?"

"Objection your honor, beyond the scope of this case. Her question is a civil matter."

Again the Judge agreed and asked the DA to move on.

"Can you take me back to the night that all of this happened. You said you had no idea she was drunk? That if you had then you would never have pursued her?"

"Yes. That is correct," Greg said into the microphone as if trying to make sure everyone heard him.

"Did you see her stumble out of the bathroom? Didn't you have a few drinks with her?"

"I did, but when I asked Jill how she was feeling, when she left the bathroom, she never said she sick or drunk. I offered to bring Mrs. Harris to the hospital and she refused. Had I know what had just happened to her I would have been more forceful and would have immediately brought her to the hospital, after calling the authorities of course." Greg said as he turned his attention to the jury instead of the DA.

"Didn't you collect her keys from the bartender?"

"I have know Jill for a long time and know that, for the most part, she is a responsible girl. I thought that she may have given the bartender her keys when she arrived," Greg finished turning his attention back to the DA.

"Even though we have testimony from the bartender, the bouncer, and other patrons that she was obviously inebriated, it is your testimony that you had no idea she was drunk and were just being a good friend?"

"The people there did not know her like I did and she seemed coherent enough. I do not know the other peoples motives, but all I know was Jill said she wanted to go home."

"Good friends... Do good friends take out restraining orders against each other? Specifically from Mrs. Harris against you."

"Objection your honor."

The revelation had brought the court into a tizzy. The press scrawled away on their pads as this new piece of gossip flew though the courtroom. Small conversations broke out through the courtroom as the Judge called both lawyers up to his desk.

"What is all this about?" The Judge asked the Ms. Alarosa.

"In high school Mrs. Harris had taken a restraining order taken out against the defendant after he refused to stop stalking her."

The Judge took the information in as Greg's lawyer broke in "Your honor, nothing ever came of that. Greg never broke it and the restraining order was dismissed. Regardless though that blemish is sealed as part of his juvenile record. She is just trying to prejudice the jury."

"Your honor I am questioning the defendants claim that they were good friends."

Sitting there the Judge weighed it. "Miss Alarosa, I am inclined to agree with Mr. Billingsly. I will tell the jury to disregard the last question and expect you to move on."

"Your honor," Ms. Alarosa began to plead.

"That is my ruling, now step back."

After the Judge's directions Ms. Alarosa, determined as ever, was allowed to continue.

"So as a good friend you brought her home. You like Jill don't you?"

"Objection your honor," Ms. Alarosa, the DA, heard over her shoulder

"It is going towards his state of mind and the relationship he has with Mrs. Harris."

"Overruled," the Judge responded back.

"Yes. I like her and have for many years now," Greg answered. "She was always a nice girl and we grew up together. I think you would be hard pressed to find a guy who did not like her in this town."

"I see and why did you like her, because she was pretty? Or was there more?"

"She is more than a pretty face. She was nice, caring, protective, loyal."

"Do you think Mrs. Harris is smart?"

"Of course."

"Responsible?"

"Most certainly or I would have never suggested my father hire her in the first place."

"I see. So you got her a job without anything in return. How nice of you."

"Your honor I do not hear a question in there," Greg's lawyer said.

"Sorry your honor, let me get back on point. Mr. Crasnick, you say that she is loyal, caring, responsible. If not you would never have liked her, let alone gotten her a position at your hospital. Is that correct?"

"Sounds right," Greg answered uneasily.

"So in your mind it is this type of person: a loyal, responsible, caring, smart person, the type of person who sleeps with another man the night her husband was re-deployed?"

Jill looked up from the floor as she felt the tide change in the courtroom. Greg gulped waiting for his lawyer. He couldn't leaving Greg out in the open, on his own.

"People change. We all know what she did when she was nineteen. ...W... Whi...While she was dating Jeff," Greg added, his school boy charm chipping away as his innocent tone turned slightly aggressive. A stutter evident.

"Are you referring to the night that she gave oral pleasures to a bouncer, patron, and officer in exchange for dropping charges filed against her?"

"Yes."

"So you think that Mrs. Harris is a woman who uses her body to get her way? Someone who uses her sexual assets and charm to manipulate men to get her way?"

"Your honor," Greg's lawyer started to object when Ms. Alarosa cut him off.

"Your honor it goes to what the defendant thought about Mrs. Harris and why he would assume that what happened between them was wanted and consensual."

The Judge nodded and told Greg he could answer.

"I think she has it in her."

"So what does she want from you then?"

Greg opened his mouth, about to say her job, but could not.

Flies came out of his mouth as Greg braced himself against his chair. The prosecutor continued her questions.

"She has not reached out for support from you. So what did she want from you? How could you help her? As you testified her history shows us that Mrs. Harris acts when she has guarantees. Did you guarantee her her job back? What did you have that she wanted? Jill has not blackmailed you in anyway. She has not even asked for her job back. You say it's lawsuit this and lawsuit that, but she has not sued the hospital for any form wrongful termination or discrimination. So again what did she want from you?"

The DA finished her question and the courtroom turned to Greg as he sweated bullets. Greg was waiting for his lawyer to intervene, but his lawyer sat mute. Looking to the Judge for support Greg found none.

"I... um... I think she.... Uh..." Greg did not know how to answer.

Jill saw right through him wondering what he had promised her that night. The DA had him she thought to herself. The entire time he had tried to play her as the victim he saved. He had played himself as the victim and now the D.A. had turned it on him. Greg could not have it both ways. Either he was her knight in shining armor or the victim.

"All I had to offer was a shoulder to cry on and a life long friendship that we shared. Something that grew into something greater that night," Greg finally answered. His face, body language, and tone betraying him. Everyone could see that Greg either knew he had forced himself on her or was holding something back now.

"I see," the Prosecutor said as she walked the courtroom before returning to her table. Leaning back on it, the DA knew Greg was exposed. With Greg on the ropes Ms. Alarosa did not back down, but pressed on one final assault.

"When you and Mrs. Harris engaged in sexual intercourse did you notice that anything was wrong with her?"

"No... it was dark. I did not see anything," Greg mumbled out still trying to regain his composure.

"I see, did you feel her body when you were in bed, what did you do exactly?"

"Yes... I touched her..."

"Where did you touch her, her face, back, her genitals?"

"Your honor is this necessary?" Greg's lawyer asked.

"Your honor Greg has told us that the situation was consensual and I think since all we have is his word the court deserves to hear what happened from him."

"I agree Miss Alarosa; however, don't overstep."

The court's attention snapped back to Greg as they watched this one-sided tennis match take shape.

"I guess I would have to say I touched her all over..."

"And you didn't notice anything wrong?"

"No"

"Really?"

"Objection your honor, asked and answered."

"Rephrase or move on Miss Alarosa," the Judge said agreeing with Greg's attorney.

"Mr. Crasnick, you testify that you did not notice anything out of normal. However, we have seen and heard medical evidence about the state that Mrs.Harris would have been in when you arrived at her home. Her breasts were sore and bruised. Her thighs and pelvic region sticky, worn, and possibly stained with blood and semen. Her vagina would have been raw and dry like sand paper. Are telling the court you did not notice any of this? You did not notice any of the bruising, the blood, or semen?"

"No I did not."

"Was this your first time having sex?"

"Objection your honor."

"I want to establish that Greg was not a virgin and had another experience to compare Mrs. Harris's state to."

"Overruled."

"So Mr. Crasnick were you a virgin that night?"

Greg bit his lip not wanting to answer, but knowing he had to.

"No." He whispered.

"What was that? The court could not hear you."

"No. I was not a virgin."

"And considering she is carrying your child it is safe to say you didn't use a condom then?" The prosecutor pushed as she got off the table and walked towards Greg, whose attitude was rising as his voice and answers got coarse and shorter.

"No I did not."

"I see… well it seems to me that the only person who wouldn't have noticed all of the abuse Mrs. Harris took was the person who raped her in that dingy bathroom bar. Do you agree? Or do you just like your women that way?"

"Objection your honor," Greg's lawyer yelled out.

"Withdrawn," the DA said with a smile as she walked back

towards her desk.

Jill smiled too. Greg was exposed for the liar and pig that he was. Greg did not have a good response or defense, an answer for the questions. For the first time in months it felt like Jill had taken back her life from that bastard. In the back of her mind though Jill wondered if there was more to his story. She wondered if there was a chance what happened was consensual and if Greg had offered her something in return for one night together. She wondered what he was still hiding in that pathetic little mind of his.

19. JOHN'S PLEA

The scene dissolved as the table's surface became cloudy and glassy before becoming solid once again.

John and Martin both leaned back in their chairs, trying to, but unable to relax, as they tried to come back to come to terms with their thoughts. Both of them had been overwhelmed at the trial and were trying to fit what had happened into their own narrative and answers.

Martin thought about the trial and what had been said. He was trying to make sense of it all and trying to figure out if Greg was guilty, if he had raped Jill twice or only once. Martin thought about how Ms. Alarosa was treated and wondered if she was unfairly treated because of her gender. Martin wondered if a male attorney would have been given more latitude and leeway.

John on the other hand couldn't shake something: he knew that girl. He didn't know where from, well other than the fact that they were clearly from the same area, but he knew her. He met her. He felt, well, he felt connected to her in some strange way.

Once they thought and when both were comfortable, they waited. They waited for the third party to guide them. However, the questions did not come. A minute passed, then two, then five and ten. Time slowed as they waited for their third partner to say something.

"Lord," John finally broke the silence. "Why do I feel so... So connected to her?"

"To who my son?"

"To Mrs. Harris?"

John's Lord smiled before answering.

"It is probably because you are tied to her. I hope you realized by now that that your accident was the one that she was at that morning. I'm sure the other connections will become clear."

As always the Entity offered more questions than answers, but his words this time gave John and Martin both an uneasy feeling.

John and Martin were a part of this story and their accident had put all of this in motion. It now became clear that time had no effect in this place and watching the trial, answering the Entity's questions told them that their involvement was more intimate to this situation than just being the cause. Jill's trial was winding down and all that was left were final statements and the jury deliberations. Looking back down to the table both John and Martin expected to see it dissolve into the courtroom; however, the table did not. Looking up they found the third chair empty. The Entity had moved behind the podium once again.

"Like the trial we have been watching our time here is coming to a close," the Entity started. "For us that means that your final statements are ahead of you. Before you give them I want you to understand how important they are. These statements impact your immediate and future fate. These statements are open ended and I implore you to speak your mind, heart, and truth. Do not tell me what you think I want to hear. After you both finish I will inform you of the verdict from our trial and your fates."

The room became tense as the stakes became real. With the Entity's words John and Martin felt as if they were opposing forces once again. That, like the trail they had watched, there would be a winning and a losing side. Someone would be right and the other wrong. Feeling their chests get heavier the Entity continued his explanation.

"For better or worse I want to know why you lived, how you lived. Why you think? How you think? I want to know where you find your truth and your ideals. If that was influenced or changed by something that happened here then let that come out as well. I know this may sound like the same thing I asked you before, but you have now had plenty of time to think, discuss, and explore your own ideals. You have had time to hear opposing views and have even had a bird's eye view of the trial that challenged you to explore your beliefs. John take a moment to finish gathering your thoughts and please begin."

Looking up at his Lord, John did not know how to begin or what to say. Sensing this his Lord encouraged him to speak again.

"I want to hear it from you again," the Entity told John trying to quell his fears. "Just be honest and speak from the heart. Tell me about your life and beliefs."

"Lord," John started tentatively. "I would never say that I did not stumble, but I would say that I let your word guide my life. I have given it a lot of thought and know that I gave you my all. I know I followed your bread crumbs and your guidance. I saw the truth in your words, in your book, and in my life. I let that guide me. Despite the other paths presented to me I never wavered. I knew your good word was the right choice and that is what I followed. I took jobs and did missions all in your name and to spread your good word. You were my inspiration and my guiding force my Lord. Your book gave me my truth and the love that I needed to make my life whole. I tried my best not to be judgmental and tried to live in your image. In your mold. Despite what I heard today and what we discussed, I do not see it differently now. I lived my life for your truth. To honor and glorify you. I lived in your grace and for your glory."

John was overtaken with emotions and teared up with nothing

more to to say. Looking towards his Lord John did not see the smile he was expecting, instead his Lord stared back at him emotionless.

"My Lord?" John asked nervously, trying to get the littlest bit of emotion out of his savior.

"My son... I am sorry, but you are not ready. You will be sent away until you are ready to present your arguments again. Please leave the court, through the back door."

The room became tense as Martin's and John's faces both fell. Martin did not know what to say or think. All he could do is watch as John's tears became harder and sadder. Without argument, fight, or disagreement, John took the command and walked towards the black, obsidian, door at the back of the courtroom.

"This is not fair," Martin yelled. "You said we would both have a chance to answer before deciding." Martin continued to yell at the Entity as he tried to understand. "How could John be dammed to hell? What did he do wrong? What chance do I have? And what is this game then? This isn't fair?"

Voicing his objections a few more times at Jesus, then Zeus, Moses, and more. Martin kept going while John, despite Martin's protests, kept walking, lost in his own thoughts.

What did I do wrong? John thought to himself as he fought through tears pouring down his face. *I was... I'm not ready? What am I missing?* John thought as he walked closer towards the obsidian door. John did not question his savior though. *Am not ready? Does that mean I get another chance?* John found himself wondering as he approached the door, wondering where he was going. If he was about to be sent to hell.

Despite Martin's objections, the Entity did not say a word as John came closer and closer to the door. Finally John was face to face with the black obsidian door.

"This isn't fair!" Martin tried yelling one more time.

John wondered where was he going and then touched the black obsidian wall, as if to push it open, when he vanished. The second he touched the wall John simply disappeared.

"He's gone..." Martin's voice fell mute of objections as John disappeared. "One-second he was here, he touched that door, and he was gone."

Turning his attention back to the podium, Martin was ready to give the Entity a piece of his mind when Jesus stopped him with a few words of his own:

"Martin, please tell me how you guided your life."

"What?" Dr. Andrews yelled at the Entity. "You expect me just to start after that?" He asked.

The Entity nodded.

Frustrated, Martin did not know what to say, how to act, or what to do. His anger was quickly replaced by apprehension and fear as he thought about the possibilities of where John had been sent. What could he say? What should he say... Where did he begin? How did he avoid the same fate?

Looking around the courtroom the images from different faiths blurred together, overwhelming his senses. Hoping to find a centering place Martin looked back to the podium and saw Zeus, no Hades. Osiris, no Saturn. Athena, Jesus, Moses, Vatu?

I'm losing it or that thing is breaking. Martin thought as he closed his eyes. So confused he had no idea where to start, but focusing on his books, his ideas, he tried to find the thought that grounded them. Once he did he began to speak.

"I let my curiosity, my search for knowledge and truth, guide me. I could not accept the popular faiths on blind trust. There was no evidence of a supernatural being, so I used my logic and my reason. I researched and pieced together. I searched for truth, for morality, for knowledge. I searched for the truth that people ascribe to a being like you and never found a faith that was without faults. So I personally searched for evidence and truth. I searched many texts and used reasoning and logic to try and find a truth. I trusted my gut and searched for knowledge. Curiosity and the search guided my life and despite what I have seen here, I would never let that change the way I lived. Even here, now, I have no idea what I am looking at or where I am. I was clearly wrong about there not being a supernatural being, but when I look back at it, at all the evidence I saw, there was nothing that pointed to this. Texts that had been rewritten, translated, and interpreted so many times that they could hardly reflect their original intent. Texts that had been used by people for evil ends were hardly reliable. So I guess in the end, and even now, I am still searching for the truth."

Martin refused to open his eyes. Seconds felt like an eternity, but when sound finally came it was from a voice that he did not recognize.

"I see... Martin please open your eyes. I am ready and honored to answer any question you have as best I can."

Not believing what he heard Martin kept his eyes closed tightly.

"Martin please just open your eyes."

20. COLOR AND LIGHT

Standing silently Martin did not know what to do or trust. His eyes had been deceiving him all day and now he did not know if his ears were deceiving him too. He was told that he won this game, but Martin was not sure he cared about that. How could this thing judge him and John or anyone else? Why did it send them through this game? And where was John? Martin would not open his eyes until he had some answers.

"Where did you send John? Did you send him to Hell?" Martin asked. His tone angry and his fists curled.

"Martin, I sent John back so he could learn more. As of Hell, that perception propagated about Hell is just a story. To me Hell is not a place, but a state of mind. Hell is ignorance, blindly following, and all of the things that come from disobedience to knowledge, truth, and honesty. I hope that where he is now will give him a chance to understand this. I hope he will see that all of the hate and problems of the world are propagated and caused by a deviation from honesty and a pure search for knowledge and the truth."

Martin still refused to open his eyes... If ignorance was Hell ,then truth and knowledge was heaven? And if heaven was a state of mind then where was he right now?

"Where exactly did you send John?" Martin pressed

"Earth. John will find himself in a new body, ready to live again.

He most likely will have no memory of what happened here or in his past life. He will get a blank slate to start from, a state where he can question and search and hopefully learn more this time than he did last."

"What about me then? Where do I go after this if I was on the right path?"

"You will also be going back to Earth in a similar state."

Anger started brewing over and Martin struck the table as he thought:

It had all been for nothing. If he was just going back, why did it matter then? Why did they have this trial if none of it mattered? Martin's emotions spilled over as he yelled out "So what is the point then! You said I did things right! Why am I going back?"

"Because you and I are not so different. You will go back with a confidence and a presence that should naturally lend you back to your current mental disposition so you can bring others along. Please Martin open your eyes, you have seen so much already, just open your eyes and take it all in."

Against his better judgment, Dr. Andrews opened his eyes and his breath was taken away. What had been luminescing marble was now fully realized colored scenes of everything that had been there before. Inlaid marble brought the scenes to a life in a beauty normally reserved for the holiest Mosques. Looking at the center podium Martin saw a variety of colors creating religious symbols at the center of the podium. Following the symbols up all Martin saw was a ball of light where the Entity used to be. The formless mass in front of him seemed to be the source of the light in the court.

"When did this happen?" Martin asked as he explored this amazing art in closer detail.

"It was there the entire time, your mind was just trying to sort it all out. Now that you have started to acknowledge what we are discussing you are able to see what was here the entire time. Your mind was processing all of it as best it could which is why you saw the images as pure light, you were confused, and now the path has been illuminated."

"What about you?" Martin said directing his question back to the ball. "You changed every time I saw you. You were Jesus, Hades, Athena, Apollo, and many others. How and why are you now just some formless luminescent light?"

"You are now seeing my true form in the way you can best understand it. During the trial you brain tried to place my form and used its own context clues to fill in the gaps. You thought that I was some type of superior being so your mind filled in the blanks by cycling through all the deities you know, trying to define my form. Now you are seeing everything clearer which is why you see me as you do now."

"But I still do not understand. How are we not that different? Did you create Earth? How did you make time pass so quickly down on Earth? Where are we? And if I am going back what is heaven?"

"I did create your world, but do not to control it. There are many beings like me in existence and your own species, mankind, are slowly evolving into a state of greater consciousness. Hopefully one day you will all join us. As for the rest of your question you would probably call me the unmoved mover or God, or Allah but my purpose is the same as yours: I am searching for a truth, just like all the beings above and below me. Time is perception. This place is a part of Earth and a part of the universe as a whole. We are on a different level of consciousness, one where the rules of time, that perception, as you know them don't apply. Many people who die come to see me, all at different states of their conscious development. Many are in a similar state as John or much worse. Every once in a while someone like you comes along.

Someone who is further along and ready to discuss these things further."

"What is heaven? Does it exist?"

"Of course it exists, it is just mislabeled. Heaven is no more than a state of mind. It is knowledge, truth. That is all. As beings you have been moving closer and closer to this state. Eventually you will learn that matter is just that. It is matter. You will learn that truth and knowledge can free you from the confines of matter, time, hate, and ignorance. It is just a matter of time until collectively your species realize this; however, until then you must go back."

All of a sudden Martin felt the mood of the conversation change. His time here was coming to a close too quickly and in an attempt to extend the conversation he asked:

"So it is Buddhism. They are most correct."

"Everyone is right. You know that. When you peel away the layers of translation and poor interpretation religion, science, and philosophy all push in a singular direction towards greater truth. As far as I know there is not a great consciousness who created this all, but then again I am not the most powerful being and am still searching. I do know that there is a search for a truth. A search for something that I and the beings above and below me are search for. One day you and your people will reach the state I am in, or possibly a more advance state, regardless you will meet hordes of beings like me doing all that we can to search for a truth. You can join us and continue the search, adding your own ideas and methods to the search."

Again the conversation felt like it was coming to a close and again Martin was not ready. He was not ready to go back. He was just starting to truly enjoy himself and now he was going to be sent back.

"Then why create Earth?"

"To learn. Through observation I learn and find out more. It is a win-win. You get life and get the ability to reach this stage one day and I get to try and find truth and knowledge though observation."

"So you can't reproduce then?" Martin carved out a question to keep things going.

"Reproduction is an odd thing. When you realize what constitutes reproduction, it is silly to ask. In your conventional terms, no we do not reproduce, but I did create a world full of beings that can so they can add billions more beings to this realm. Do you have any more questions before our session here ends?"

The Entity had noticed Martin's push away from the end and had acknowledged what Martin did not want to. This time was coming to an end and Martin could not think of anything. He wanted to sit in this place forever, to think, to take it all in, but he had a feeling that that was not an option now, but maybe one day. Looking at the empty desk next to him Martin's eyes wandered to the space where the table used to sit and a thought came to him.

"How does it all end for Jill?"

"That is something you will find out first hand. It has not happened yet so I have no have no idea? Anything else?"

"What actually happened to Jill? Who actually raped her? What actually happened that night?"

"That is something I can show you. Come back to the table and watch before you go back."

21. THE WHOLE STORY

Jill was standing at the vanity in the dingy bar bathroom and, with a bird's eye view, Martin knew that her rapist was about to walk in. Martin cringed as the door opened as he waited to see Greg and Andrew.

And it was not Greg though. Standing behind Jill was one of the hooligans that had been schooled at pool earlier. He was standing behind her undoing his fly.

How horrible. Martin thought as the door opened and the other two entered.

In an instant one of the new guys pushed Jill down into the sink as the other new entry pulled her pants and panties off. Then the hooligan who entered first penetrated her, calling her a "little bitch"as he did.

This scene unfolded for about ten minutes as the three of them had their way with her. One of them would control her, while the other two took advantage. Jill had no way of knowing who did this to her or even how many. Watching this horrible scene unfold Martin felt pity for Jill. There was no way she could have ever known it was three guys, the way that they performed their assault it could have just as easily been two or five.

After they finished they threw her panties at her and disappeared. Jill threw the panties away as the three rapist slipped out the back door. Jill was no wiser to what they had done.

A minute or two later Greg walked through the back door as Jill exited the bathroom. Martin felt his stomach drop as he realized one thing: Greg was innocent. Greg took hold of Jill as she fell out of the bathroom and helped her back to the bar. It was all like he described. Greg got her keys, helped her into her car, and he and Andrew parted ways. Now Martin wondered if Greg was telling the truth about the rest.

As the car drove away the scene changed, Martin now had bird's eye view of Jill's bedroom. Jill was on the bed crying when Greg walked in and took a seat next to her.

"What is it Jill?" Greg asked as he placed his hand on her mid back.

"It's fucking everything... Mr. Witherspoons death. Jeff's deployment. My suspension.. And... And ... It's too damn much for one person to take," Jill answered. In the back of Martin's mind he wondered if Jill was holding back, if she had remembered the rape.

"It's okay Jill," Greg tried to console her. "I know the leak was not your fault... It's okay," Greg finished as he moved his hand to the small of her back.

Jill broke through her tears and the drinks, her eyes fully awake and her mind clear. "How do you know?" she asked cooly as she scooted away from Greg.

"Well, I know who leaked it. I think you and I could work something out if you really want your job back," Greg responded as he placed his hand on her thigh.

The tension between them grew as it all clicked in Jill's mind.

"You bastard...You leaked it," Jill screamed as she rose from the bed. "You think that you can cost me my job and then come in here and blackmail me? You will never get away with this you little asshole. Leave now." Walking to her bedroom door Jill threw it open for Greg to leave.

"If I leave, you will never work in this town again. I hold all the cards here Jill. So if you want this to all blow over sit down and listen."

Jill did not move, but did shut the door. She was going to hear what he had to say.

"Good girl, now let's think about this. You are a little slut in the eyes of the law and everyone who saw the two of us leave together. In one letter I can make sure your husband finds out about our night together. I can make sure he finds out about the little cheating slut you are. I'm sure these deployments aren't easy on a marriage."

Jill swallowed hard as she began to see how much control Greg wielded.

"Beyond your marriage if you are a pain tonight things will get much worse. I will make sure you are found guilty of any indiscretion or crime leading from the accident last night. You will never work in the medical field again and I will personally make sure that you are punished to the fullest extent of the law. You will be penniless, single, and, with a little luck, in prison. Your little town will turn against you and your life will be over. Of course you can change all that if you come over here and sit down next to me."

Seeing how screwed she could be Jill took control of her fate and walked back to the bed.

"Good... Jill... Good."

"What do you want?" Jill asked Greg as she stood in front of him.

"I think you know exactly what I want. You can start on your knees and we can develop from there."

Sitting above the situation Martin wondered how Jill did not remember any part of this.

Jill was on her knees, her hands on Greg's waistband as she prepared for the worst. Nervous, shaking with fear, anger, and frustration Jill undid his belt and started to pull off his pants when Greg stopped her.

"This is a little stiff," Greg started. "Look how bout you get in bed and get those clothes off, I'll go get us another drink and maybe it will loosen you up. We should enjoy this night together."

As much as she wanted to fight, Jill just silently nodded and started to strip as Greg left the room. Martin followed Greg and watched him pour two glasses of wine. After the glasses were poured he spiked Jill's before he bringing it back to the room.

The little bastard. Martin thought. *He did drug her and she washed the wrong glass.*

Jill took her drink in one gulp and they started. Jill was obviously not herself and as Martin watched Greg take advantage of her all he could think was that Greg deserved whatever punishment he got. The bastard was too much of a pig to notice the blood or bruises. He was so worried about her remembering this that he possibly made Jill forget her other assailants. His own greed and stupidity led to the charges against him. He had no one to blame but himself.

Andrew.... The thought hit Martin like a ton of bricks knocking any smile off of his face. Greg may have deserved what he got, but Andrew was completely innocent. He had done nothing wrong other than being friends with Greg.

Turning back to the memory, an hour after they started they finished. Greg showered, dressed, and left. Jill was sound asleep as Greg closed the door behind him. As the scene ended Martin tried to peel himself away from the table, back into the courtroom, but he could not. Instead he found himself surrounded by darkness. Martin could not move, but instead watched as a distant light came closer. Blinding him as Martin struggled to hold onto everything he had ever learned or knew. Trying to hold onto the courtroom and his identity as Martin felt it all slip away.

22. TWINS

"Push… Just a little more. Push," the doctor told Jill. "Come on. Just a little bit more and then you will be done. Come on, your first boy is good, just one more push and let's give him a little brother or sister."

With a scream Jill gave one more push and heard the cries of another baby.

"It's another boy. Let's get them cleaned up so you can hold them."

Jill looked around the room exhausted. Her mother and father were at her side because her husband was overseas still. Pain hit her as she thought about raising her rapist's baby instead of Jeff's. She had told Jeff everything once the paternity test came back. Their relationship was still strained, but Jill prayed that when he came home they could fix the damage. Even though she could, she did not want to raise the kids alone.

Those thoughts and troubles disappeared when the doctor handed her two bundles of life. Full of joy Jill looked at her boys and thought about everything that had led to this. Tears of joy and sorrow ran down her face as months of pain and anguish finished in something so beautiful.

Two months ago Greg and Andrew had been convicted and sentenced. The jury was out for a few days, but in the end justice had been served. After the criminal trial the civil suit was settled quickly. Jill was awarded sole custody of these two boys, Greg and his family provided her a healthy settlement and would pay child support. They started a college fund for both children and even purchased her and the boys, a house and a new car. After everything that had happened Greg's family was trying to make amends. Jill hoped that it was not all for show and that one day they could be part of the boys life.

Jill could not help but smile, she was so happy that she had made it through. The nightmare was over and Jill was ready to raise her children. That gave her hope, hope that she had not had in a long time.

"What is it buddy?" Jill said to one of her boys as Jill's mother took his sleeping brother.

Reaching towards her, the boy looked like he was reaching past her trying to catch a fleeting memory before it disappeared.

"You look like you know something little guy. Hmm what is it that you know?" Jill asked as she tickled his little stomach.

Laughing, the little guy flailed in her arms as he reached for and then hugged his mother for the first time.

"Do you have names?" Jill's mother asked her daughter as Jill embraced her child.

"Yeah I think so," Jill responded. "The little guy in your arms will be Jonathan, after Mr. Witherspoon. This little guy will be Luther, like Dr. King, because he seems like he can see something the rest of us can't. "

And that was how Jonathan and Luther started their lives anew, as brothers. Both trials were over and the new family was ready to search for truth, knowledge, and love that they could bring to us all.

Thank you for reading Trial. I hope this book has, if nothing else, given you a place to start or continue your own search for truth and knowledge. This is one of my first types of books in what I describe as philosophical fiction or narrative philosophy. I hope you enjoyed it and will read my other works that attempt to dive into philosophical issues with an approachable narrative spin.

If you enjoyed this book you can can find my other published works @:

DCREED.org

@DC_REEd (Instagram)

dcreedpublishing (Facebook)

Follow, like, and subscribe for all of the latest publishing news related to D.C. Reed.

ACKNOWLEDGEMENT

Figuring out who to honor here is harder than I thought it would be. The list is either insanely long or short depending on how you look at it.

I'm going to start by thanking my readers. I write for each and every single one of you. If one person, a hundred, or a hundred thousand read this book, know that it was worth it because you picked it up. I hope that it challenged you to think, I hope you enjoyed it, and if you did please share it with someone else you think would enjoy.

I would like to thank my brother, who probably doesn't realize that he was the one who came up with the idea for this book many many years ago. It was his inspiration to have a trial about the afterlife, before a deity or being that spurred this novel.

I would like to thank my mother and my wife. The two people who have stood by me, read through these, and helped me shape Trial into what it became. They are the ones who deal with my insecurity, my issues, and the pain of being an author and without them it wouldn't have been possible.

I would like to of course than my editors, who helped me make this book into something that someone would want to and be able to read. I had a few and they deserve their praise.

Finally, I would like to thank my friends, family, beta readers, and all the people who told me to keep going. Writing the story is the easy part. Getting over your own fear is the hard part. All of those people, whether you know it or not helped push me to this point where this work is available for the world to see.

Thank you for your time

D.C. Reed

ABOUT THE AUTHOR

D.c. Reed

As a philosophy (ethics) and music graduate of the University of North Florida D.C. Reed is an aspiring writer and teacher who has written for sports outlets, religion nerd and presented papers at university conferences in the south east. Currently living with his wife and two dogs in Atlanta Ga. D.C. strives to write stories that present complex ideals through engaging narratives. He believes that Philosophy is one of the most useful and avoided subjects. Normally limited to 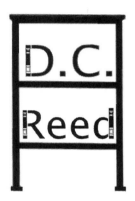 those in higher education D.C. Reed strives to bring these issues to life through stories, essays, and other writings so everyone can engage them.

Made in the USA
Columbia, SC
25 May 2023

16879282R00076